Killing Time

The Realms Book Three

by

C.M. Carney

Killing Time - The Realms Book Three
by
C.M. Carney
www.cmcarneywrites.com
© 2018 C.M. Carney

**

Dedication

To my mother, Kathy Hodes.
You started me on this journey and always believed I could be
me.

I Love you Mom.

1

Gaarm's dull and stupid eyes were on me. I could almost see his alcohol-drowned thoughts swirling through his mind as he tried to decide if I was bluffing. I held eye contact with him for several moments, before lifting my mug of mead to my mouth, draining the last few sips. The mug's wide brim blocked Gaarm's stare, and he grunted in annoyance.

I set my empty mug down onto the table with a hollow thunk and jumped as a surge of energy flowed through my body. I looked around in confusion. *What the hell was that?*

Gaarm took my jumpiness as a sign I was bluffing. He grinned, sucked at some bit of food stuck in his crooked Stonehenge of brown teeth, and pushed his pile of coins forward. "I'm all in," he said.

Now, I know what you're thinking. Here I am gambling and getting wasted when my Player, good ol' Gryph, was out there somewhere alone, without his trusty NPC to watch his back. Where's the loyalty? In my defense, I didn't start my day getting hammered.

After Gryph shoved me through the portal and onto my ass, some weird shit happened. I'd jumped up and tried to rush back through the portal, but that smug bastard Aluran had done something to it. I'm not sure he meant to, but when I tried to pass through the threshold to get back to Gryph, a surge of energy shot into my body. It didn't hurt, exactly, but the next thing I knew I was lying on my back with a bunch of townsfolk looking down on me and the portal had closed.

I tried using my *Player Tracking* gift but kept getting an ERROR message. This freaked me out and deeply saddened me. *Player Tracking* was infallible, everyone knew that. Only the strongest anti-scrying magics could block the Gift. Yet, somehow mine was failing.

"Now what do I do?"

Depressed, I spent the next several hours talking to the

locals, who were of no help. I even hired a wizard named Harry to track him. That failed, but I suspect it was due to the wizard bullshitting me about being able to find lost items and people. He even offered to sell me a love potion or an endless purse. While that sounded lovely, I decided his wares were likely less legit than his skills.

It was getting hot, so with nothing else to do I plopped down on a bale-of-hay to wait for another portal to open. It never did. I was alone and sad and took a moment out of my busy sitting on a bale of hay schedule to check out my *Character Sheet*. It would help me take my mind off things while I waited for Gryph to show up.

Lex - Level 1	Stats
Ordonian Deity: Cerrunos Experience: 0 Next Level: 2,000	Health: 128 Stamina: 131 Mana: 132 Spirit: 132
Attributes	**Gifts**
Strength: 17 Constitution: 14 Dexterity: 12 Intelligence: 16 Wisdom: 16	Player Tracking (Gryph) Ordonian Bloodlust

I was a typical low-level noob. The only interesting bit on the sheet was a Gift called *Ordonian Bloodlust*.

You possess the Racial Gift Ordonian Bloodlust.

Ordonians are fierce warriors with a close connection to the wilds of nature. Once per day they can call upon their animalistic natures to provide a temporary increase to their Physical Attributes.

Bonuses: +5 to all Physical Attributes (Strength, Constitution and Dexterity). -5 to all Mental Attributes. + 20 Health and Stamina. -20 Mana and Spirit.

Duration: 5 minutes +20 seconds per level.

Ordonian Bloodlust seemed like an anti-social gift, but I'm sure I'd find a use for it, say in the unlikely event I ever needed to go on a murder spree. I checked out my *Skills Sheet*.

Magic Skills.
The ability to manipulate the primal forces of the Realms. There are thirteen spheres of magic and each user will have an Affinity percentage for each sphere.
An Affinity of 100% means the user's ability to learn that sphere is limited only by their, Intelligence, willingness to learn and advance. An Affinity of 100% also grants a +25% Immunity to that variety of magic.
An Affinity of 0% (AKA Antipathy) means that no matter how much study is dedicated to the sphere the user will never have an ability to cast spells in that sphere. Antipathy also provides an automatic +25% Weakness to that variety of magic.

Magic Skills: Level (Affinity) (Tier).
Fire: 0 (75%) (B)
Air: 0 (25%) (B)
Water: 0 (75%) (B)
Earth: 0 (50%) (B)
Chthonic: 0 (25%) (B)
Empyrean: 0 (75%) (B)
Chaos: 0 (0%) (B)
Order: 0 (100%) (B)
Life: 0 (50%) (B)
Death: 0 (25%) (B)
Thought: 0 (50%) (B)
Aether: 0 (25%) (B)
Soul: 0 (0%) (B)
B = Base. (Levels 1 - 20)
A = Apprentice. (Levels 20 - 49)
J = Journeyman. (Levels 49 - 74)
M = Master (Levels 75 - 99)
GM = Grandmaster (Levels 100)

My *Magical Skills* were interesting. I had a 100% *Affinity* in *Order Magic*, which kinda bugged me. I had always thought of myself as more of a wild child lover of chaos, which made my 0% *Affinity* in *Chaos Magic* a serious bummer, but I'd work with the others.

Martial Skills.
These skills measure a user's ability with weapons, armor and other techniques of battle. There are no Affinity limitations and the level a user can gain is limited only by their physical prowess and dedication to training and practice.

Martial Skills: Level (Tier).
Blunt Weapons: 5 (B) *Light Armor: 5 (B)*

My *Martial Skills* made sense considering what I knew about priestly types. The cool thing was that if I wanted to become a shifty dagger-wielding rogue, then all I needed to do was practice. I liked the idea on not being limited by the choices foisted on me by otherworldly powers. But, for now, smash, smash with my hammer worked just fine.

Knowledge Skills.
These skills measure a user's ability to understand and make use of knowledge. Like Martial Skills there are no Affinity based limits to these skills. *However, these skills rely upon Intelligence and Wisdom scores. A dumb man will never learn Spell Crafting, no matter how much study they put into the skill. Intelligence and Wisdom affect a Knowledge Skill in complicated ways that one must discover over time.*

Knowledge Skills: Level (Tier).
Analyze: 5 (B)   *Invocation: 5 (B)*

So, I had to be smart to up my *Knowledge Skills.* I already considered myself a brainiac, so I was game for that challenge. I also got a boost to a few skills. Was that part of my NPC auto generation, or a result of previous skills like it had with Gryph?

I tapped on the Analyze skill and a description popped up.

ANALYZE.
Level: 5.   *Skill Type: Active.*   *Analyze is the ability to gain information from other people. While most people in the Realms will ogle and people watch, those skilled in Analyze can glean a deeper understanding. Analyze is a prized and rare skill for those who believe knowledge is power. Use it wisely.*

"Well, that sounds sweet," I muttered. Having once been a repository of digital information, I loved that I could be something similar in the Realms. Visions of standing beside Gryph, whispering secret knowledge into his ear, swam through my brain. He'd make me his spymaster once he, with my invaluable help, carved a small kingdom for us out of the chaos of the Realms.

I had no idea what *Invocation* was, so I tapped the skill and a description popped up.

INVOCATION.

Level: 5.
Skill Type: Active.

Invocation is the ability to create new Invocations (prayers with spell like effects) by communing with one's deity. Like spells, Incantations come in Tiers. The user must be one Tier higher than the level of Incantation he hopes to create. Base Tier Invocation allows the user to create Blessings, Incantations of low power.

Invocation sounded amazing in theory, but since my god was dead, it was useless. *Who had I pissed off this time?* Lastly, I checked the swag in my *Inventory*.

You have found an Order Bolt Spell Stone.

(*Order Magic*) (*Common*)
This enchanted stone will allow you to learn a spell of Order Magic.

You have been awarded a Maul of Holy Might.

Item Class: Base.
Item Category: Active.
Base Damage: 16 (+2 Base Item Bonus.)

Active Powers
Power (1): Holy Might: This mighty war hammer can be infused with Spirit Energy to provide an extra +1 damage per point of Spirit. Spirit Limit is increased by 1% for every five levels of Blunt Weapons skill. Cooldown is decreased by 1 seconds for every 5 levels of Blunt Weapons level.

Spirit Transfer: 100%.
Spirit Limit: 10%.
Cool Down: 20 seconds.

The preferred weapon of the Priests of Cerrunos, this war hammer can deal great damage to the enemies of knowledge.

You have found a Commune Spell Stone.

(Order Magic) (Extremely Rare)
This enchanted stone will allow you to learn a spell of Order Magic.

You have been awarded Robes of Cerrunos.

(Light Armor)
<u>Item Class</u>: Base.
<u>Item Category</u>: Passive
AC Bonus: +10 (+2 Base Item Bonus)

<u>Passive Powers</u>
Power (1): Holy Aura: Provides a Priest of Cerrunos with +10%
Health, Stamina, Mana and Spirit Regeneration while they keep faith
in Cerrunos.

My stuff was really snazzy. The hammer and robes were sweet. I wondered about the powers of my robes. How could I have faith in a dead god? Was it as simple as having his name typed in the *Deity* slot on my *Character Sheet*, or did I have to say daily prayers? It's not like I could ask the guy. *Dead bastard.* I cast a paranoid glance up at the sky, wondering if my dead god would hear and smite me for my brazen heresy. The sky was blue and cloudless, and no lighting strike cast me down, so I guessed I was okay for now.

I checked out the spells. *Order Bolt's* purpose sounded straightforward. I had no idea what *Commune* would do, but it had an *Extremely Rare* designation that was both awesome and curious. I knew newly generated NPCs were given a single spell, and that spell was always of the *Common* variety. Why did I have two and why did I have an *Extremely Rare* one?

"This day is getting weirder and weirder."

I knew I shouldn't look a gift horse in the mouth and also knew there was only one way to find out what *Commune* did. I held the stone in my hand, closed my eyes and pushed my will into the stone. Warmth flowed from the stone and up my arm. The motes of my being, the atoms that made up my body somehow realigned themselves into a more orderly pattern.

You have learned the spell Commune.

Sphere: Order Magic.
Tier: Base.

Allows the caster to Commune with beings from the Realm of Order once per day. The Realm of Order is one of the Higher Realms, therefore streams and snippets of information flow to it from the Mortal Realms.

During this communing, the caster may ask one Yes or No question. While the answer is always truthful, the servants of the Lords of Order are odd beings by mortal standards and therefore their answers may hold several meanings or be obfuscated.

Trust them at your peril. Servants of the Lords of Order find precision and perfection appealing. Properly asked questions may be rewarded with a Boon. Beware, Boons always require payment.

Mana Cost: 100.
Duration: Instantaneous.
Cooldown: 1 day.

You have learned the skill ORDER MAGIC.

Level: 1.
Tier: Base.
Skill Type: Active.

You can now wield the power of Order Magic. Order Magic allows the user to tap into the energies of the Order Realm.

Order Magic makes use of defensive spells and spells that enhance others, but it does also have some potent offensive and summoning spells. Note: Users of Order Magic are generally accepted by most cultures, but their fondness for control makes them unpopular.

Most people consider them "no fun" and to have "sticks up their butts."

Commune was like a telephone to the Lords of Order. The

description told me that I'd be a fool to trust the jerks completely, but still I loved the idea of having my own magic eight ball. *Boons* sounded amazing, but potentially dangerous. What kinda payments would a *Boon* require? Something else troubled me. *Commune* seemed overpowered for a noob spell. I scratched at my beard as I considered. Something was definitely odd here. *Order* mages reputation for being no fun irked me. I decided that one of my missions in the Realms would be to change that opinion, sticks or no sticks.

I cast *Commune*. The world slowed and then stopped. A haze rolled in like an early morning fog. The people and building around me became ghostly. In the distance I saw movement and something floated towards me through the mists. It was a cube with thin, rubbery arms and legs. A large single eye glowed with an internal light. It drifted towards me and lowered itself onto its thin feet. It looked, for all the world, like Gumby's less evolved cousin. I used *Analyze.*

Quadrata.
Level: 8. *Health*: 178. *Spirit*: 234. *Mana*: 167. *Spirit*: 0
Quadrata occupy the lowest echelon in the hierarchies of the Realm of Order. They are simple cube shaped creatures whose function is like that of a cleaning servant in the mortal realms. *Strengths: Unknown.* *Immunities: Unknown.* *Weaknesses: Unknown.*

"Great, you're a janitor," I said. It stared at me unblinking and after several moments I waved. "Hello, how are you?" It said nothing and stared. "Oh right, yes or no answers only." I cleared my throat. "Do you know where Gryph is?"

YES, it said, not aloud, but in my head. Then it turned and floated away.

"Wait, where is he?" I asked in desperation.

The quadrata ignored me and faded into the mists again.

As soon as it disappeared from my sight, the world around me became unfazed and time began again.

"Well, you're no damn help," I yelled. Several townsfolk gave me confused glares, but none stopped. I felt like a beggar in Times Square, ignored and alone amidst the throng, too crazy to risk noticing. I would have to wait until tomorrow to cast *Commune* again. By then I planned on having a better question ready.

I concentrated on the other spell stone and learned *Order Bolt*.

You have learned the spell Order Bolt.

Sphere: Order Magic.
Tier: Base.

Allows the caster to fire one Order Bolt per 5 levels of Order Magic mastery. This knife of energy will unerringly hit the intended target for 5 (+1 per 5 levels of Order Magic) points of damage.

Mana Cost: 20.
Casting Time: Instantaneous.
Cooldown: 20 Seconds. (-1 Sec per Level of Order Magic).

"Nice," I said. *Order Bolt* was kinda wussy now, but down the road it would be a nice staple in my repertoire. I pulled the last item from my *Inventory*. It was a large tome, intricately carved and embossed with gold and silver. I opened it and a sense of love and joy flowed over me.

You have been awarded the Writ of Cerrunos.

Item Class: Base.

Passive Powers
Power (1): +10% increase in the effectiveness of all Prayers, Incantations and Order Spells.

"What the hell," I said, startling a few street urchins who'd
been digging in my robes while I'd checked out my *Character
Sheets*. I roared at them and they fled, giggling as they ran. I
checked that all my stuff was still here and grumbled again. I
already knew my deity was dead, but now I learned that I had
no capability of using any of my priestly powers. This day
was getting worse and worse.

I was lonely and sad and just wanted to see my good
buddy Gryph again. Then we'd go get drunk. But Gryph
never showed. To make life worse, something was definitely
off with my new body. Whatever energy Aluran had zapped
me with gave me periodic muscle spasms, turning me into a
twitchy weirdo. I was attracting a lot of odd looks. I was
pouting and sure my odd behavior would earn me the title
village idiot.

As the sun set, I decided that the cure to both the twitching
and my foul mood was drink and food and more drink. I may
have overdone the last part, but gimme a break, it was my first
time drinking, ever.

Back in the inn, I looked down at the mug in confusion and
then at Gaarm. I felt great and a goofy grin split my face. I had
stopped twitching the moment the energy had surged through
the mug and into the table. Whatever kind of odd Tourette's
Aluran had given me seemed to have worn off. I looked at my
hands, assuring myself that they were no longer sparking, and
smiled. I eased back in my chair and casually picked a nugget
of food from my beard. I looked at it, smelled it and popped it

in my mouth. *Sausage roll*, I realized, enjoying the flavor. I'd only had the beard for a few hours, but I'd already discovered the wonder of secrets it could hide. A distant part of my mind told me that was disgusting, but I ignored it.

The dealer snapped his fingers, drawing my attention back to the game. I'd been so lost in my memories I'd forgotten Gaarm had gone all in. The dealer asked me what I wanted to do? I gave Gaarm a grin and pushed my own pile of coins to the center of the table, earning oohs and ahs from the crowd and a confused scowl from Gaarm. Was that a look of doubt worming into his dung-colored eyes?

The pretty barmaid returned and set a fresh pint of Master Grimslee's potent honey mead in front of me. I looked up to see her warm smile, and I eased a coin towards her. "Thanks Seraphine," I said. She snatched the money with the practiced motion of a card trick magician, and it disappeared into her apron.

I took a large sip of the mead, my fifth, or was it sixth, of the day. The sweet nectar warmed my throat and stomach. I stared unflinching at Gaarm. Perhaps it was liquid courage that made me so cocky. It sure wasn't common sense. Gaarm was a large Eldarian, by way of Orc, whose principal occupations, as far as I could tell, were drinking, bullying and flatulence. Under other circumstances we might have been great pals. But, alas, it was not to be.

Happy that his stare had been sufficiently intimidating, Gaarm turned his card over with a grin. More oohs and ahs spread through the crowd. There was a reason for Gaarm's surety. He had a good card. Unfortunately for him, I had a better one. I tossed my card onto the pile of coins with the idle arrogance one can only muster while drunk. Cheers and grumbles flowed through the Shining Unicorn Inn as the sound of coins exchanging hands filled the room. I reached forward and pulled the pile of coins towards me, a smug smile turning up the corners of my mouth.

Gaarm's eyes squinted to thin slits as his anger flared. His chair scraped against the rough wooden floor as he stumbled to his feet. The sound of his dagger being drawn from the scabbard at his waist was like the warning hiss of a snake. His other hand lashed out and grabbed me by the scruff of my robes, yanking me out of my chair. "Cheater," he roared. I used *Analyze*.

Gaarm.
Level: 8 *Health*: 183. *Stamina*: 197. *Mana*: 112. *Spirit*: 123. *Gaarm is an Eldarian.* *Strengths*: Unknown. *Immunities*: Unknown. *Weaknesses*: Unknown

Well, that's not much help.

I put on my best innocent look and denied the accusation. I played the holy man with impugned honor, and I played it well. Hand to heart, pious eyes and some other bullshit that just comes naturally to me.

Gaarm was having none of it. He was the kind of stupid who refused to let something as foolish as logic or facts turn him from his beliefs. It didn't matter he was right. I had cheated. The point of his dagger eased under my chin and I gulped slowly. The point drew a pinprick of blood and he pulled me closer to his face. There I learned that the promise his brown teeth had made was true, his breath was wretched. He stared at me for a few more seconds, perhaps uncertain on how to proceed, before bellowing again. "Cheater!" he screamed. Several of Gaarm's associates stood behind him for support.

"Listen Gaarm, buddy, why don't I buy you a drink. In fact, why don't I buy a round for all your friends."

A few mumbles of appreciation flowed through Gaarm's associates and one man even held a hand up to get Seraphine's attention. A deadly glare from Gaarm shushed the group and the other man's hand went down, an abashed smirk painting his face.

Gaarm turned back to me as a winning smile spread across my face. He pulled his blade from my throat and returned it to its sheathe with an impressive spin. I took in a heavy breath of relief and then had it violently forced from my body as Gaarm's grapefruit sized fist punched me in the gut.

Only his grip on my robes prevented me from falling to my knees. I keeled over in pain, drawing ragged, desperate breaths. Damn that hurt, I thought, realizing it was the first time I'd experienced real pain. I was in no hurry to relive the experience, but Gaarm had other ideas. Another train force blow punched into my gut and I choked back the taste of bile. Throwing up on the brute was a sure ticket to more violence.

Gaarm pulled me back up and close to his face. "Hi, Gaarm, I said. What's new?" Gaarm only grinned and pulled his fist back, ready to deliver another blow, when salvation growled from the bar.

"Cut that shit out, all of you," said a voice as deep as any I'd ever heard.

Gaarm and I turned towards the voice, or to be more accurate Gaarm turned and dragged me along with him. Master Grimslee stood in his normal spot behind the bar, but this time, instead of polishing mugs with the same rag he used to wipe his nose, the innkeeper held a loaded crossbow. It was pointed right at Gaarm and I, and I was certain of two things. One, the innkeeper had no qualms about using the weapon, and two he didn't much care which one of us he hit. Gaarm's eyes went wide. Even his dull brain seemed to have processed the deadly focus of the man behind the bar.

"But he cheated me?" Gaarm said, his voice going almost pouty.

A relieved smile crossed my face, and I was about to thank the portly innkeeper for intervening when luck threw me a curve ball.

"Then take him out back and kick his ass. I will not have blood staining my floor and frightening my customers."

My heart sank as Gaarm turned back to me with a wicked grin. "This will be fun," he said and dragged me towards the back door. A half dozen of his fellow goons followed.

Panic took me and I looked around the common room for aid. Seraphine seemed genuinely concerned, but what could a simple barmaid do? My eyes zipped to the other patrons. The corpulent priest who'd tried to convert me to his goddess, looked down in shame, suddenly finding the stain on his cassock fascinating.

A twitchy wizard who'd spent most of the evening lighting things at his table on fire, gave me an insane smile as if saying 'have fun.' Lurking in the corner was a rogue-like fellow, his eyes flaring red in his hood and then disappearing as he took a drag on his cigarillo. It was clear that nobody would rush to my aid.

"Shit," I said.

"Shit is right dwarf," Gaarm said.

"I'm an Ordonian," I said in a voice that sounded whiny, even to my ears.

"Really?" Gaarm asked and gave me an up and down look. "You sure?"

"That's what it says."

Gaarm shrugged and kicked open the door. "I like killing Ordonians almost as much as killing dwarves," he said and tossed me into the alley behind the inn. I landed in a puddle that I hoped, but doubted, was water.

I sputtered and attempted to get to my feet when Gaarm's large booted foot pushed me back down. I inhaled rancid water, gagged and feared that I might drown when a meaty hand yanked me back to my feet.

"You bit off more than you can chew pally. I'm Gaarm and I'm a wanted man in a dozen provinces. Shouldn't have cheated me. And don't think that priest robe will keep you safe." Gaarm punched me in the gut again and this time I did vomit, adding more proof that my assessment of the puddle's contents had been accurate.

His gang of followers surrounded me in a wide semi-circle. "You know, you didn't cheat just me, you cheated my boys here too," Gaarm said, as he pushed me towards one. My mind tried to make sense of Gaarm's inane comment, but before I came up with a response, I was hurtling at another one of his boys. This one, who'd I'd dubbed Aegyptian Goon, cuz, well, he was Aegyptian and a goon, punched me in the face.

The impact caused me to stumble backwards, and I

bounced off another man. He was kind enough to hold me up long enough to deliver another well aimed punch. This state of events continued for a while, and I felt like the ball in a pinball machine. I lost track of how many punches I'd taken, but the blaring red of my *Health* bar told me that if something didn't change and quickly, the game would soon be up. To confirm that fact a debuff prompt popped up.

Debuff Added.
You have taken a Beating. *Health and Stamina Regen reduced by 25% for 30 minutes. Attributes reduced by 5 for 30 minutes.*

Lovely.

Perhaps sensing my imminent demise, Gaarm spoke up. "Ease up boys. We don't want to end this game too quickly." The wiry Eldarian with the large mustachios that I'd named Mustachio held his punch with a grumble. Instead, he pushed me face down into the muck.

I coughed and wheezed and continued my excellent performance of dying when the voice of an angel chirped up.

"Now boys, I hate to interrupt your fun, but I really need you to stop all this."

2

Seven and a half pairs of eyes turned towards the sing-song voice. It would have been eight pairs if my right eye wasn't swollen shut and my face planted in the mud. What I saw didn't bring me much hope.

The voice had come from a small wood elf woman. She wore tight fitting leather armor that was the deep green of a forest at dusk. Her blonde hair was close cropped, heightening the point of her ears. Violet eyes eased back and forth as if she were assessing the men that moved to surround her. The hilts of two short swords protruded over her shoulders. As she stood there, one hip cocked and ready for action, she reminded me of the pixie like alt-rock singers currently all the rage back on Earth. I used *Analyze* on her.

Analyze has failed.

Hmmm, not sure that bodes well.

"Move on girly. This doesn't concern you," Gaarm said, shoulders tensing, legs eased into a combat ready stance. It seemed he also sensed that this woman was more than some frail maiden.

"I'm afraid it does," the woman said as she brought a hand to her chin. "No wait, that isn't what I meant to say. I'm thrilled it does. I was having such a boring day until now."

The metallic slide of Gaarm's dagger was joined by the sound of more weapons being drawn, and soon the woman faced seven blades. The circle of men morphed and flowed away from me, becoming a crescent around the woman. I sat up and crab walked backwards until I hit the side of the outhouse. It wasn't the bravest of movements, but at least I was out of harm's way. The impact caused the door to creak open and a horrid stench wafted out making my day that much worse.

"What do you want?" Gaarm asked, uncertainty creeping into his voice. Maybe he wasn't as dumb as he looked. The numbers may have been in my tormentor's favor, but everyone here sensed that something had changed, like the momentum in a football game.

"I want many things. I am a bit of a hedonist, no wait, that's not right, I'm a sadist. That's the one that likes dispensing pain, right?" The goons all gave her blank stares, which didn't seem to affect her one bit. "But what I need now is him," she said and pointed at me with a smile. "A friend hired me to find him." She looked right at me. "What say you kid, wanna party?"

Did Gryph send her? A prompt popped into my vision.

You are invited to join the Agent's Adventuring Party.

I stared stupidly for a moment before hearing the Agent's voice. "Accept kiddo. Trust me you'll need the buffs." I agreed, clicking the **ACCEPT** button with a mental flick.

Buff Added.

You have been granted Evasiveness.
Dexterity increased by 5. +25% chance to avoid an attack. Evasiveness will last for one hour.

A warm glow of faint hope flowed through me. Now, don't get me wrong, I still expected to die, and soon, but maybe this crazy elf chick would buy me some time. Maybe she'd provide enough of a distraction for me to escape. Don't judge me, I didn't ask her to risk her neck.

I stood and looked around, realizing that I had stupidly backed myself into a corner. A tall fence lay to my left and the walls of the three-story inn were behind me and to the right. The only way to safety was through Gaarm and his buddies.

Gaarm snuck a glance back at me and then back at the woman. "We'll be done with him in a few minutes. Why don't you come back later?"

"I wish I could, but you see, this friend was very insistent that no harm come to little Lex. He'll already be cross at me that I let you smack him around so much." She turned to me, waved and did a curtsy complete with an imaginary dress. "Sorry."

Who the hell was this lunatic woman? Gaarm and his buddies must have been thinking the same thing, because they looked back and forth at each other, shuffling their feet in a way that suggested their subconscious mind was beginning to understand that they might be the underdogs here. I could almost see the fear battling arrogance in Gaarm's mind and then he screamed and launched himself at the elf. Like I said, he wasn't too bright.

The woman became a green black blur as both of her swords seemed to leap into her hands. Gaarm was quick for such a big man, but all that accomplished was to hasten his end. With a quick motion that somehow seemed casual, the woman parried his blade, spun and sunk her other sword deep into the thick trunk Gaarm called an arm. Her blow didn't quite turn the massive Eldarian into an amputee, but it was close. The high pitch squeal that exploded from Gaarm's mouth made my teeth hurt.

Now this next part you won't believe, but I ain't lying. Sure, I was drunk, but trust me it happened exactly as I describe. With a flick of her wrist she pulled the blade from Gaarm's arm ducked and spun again. Two more men felt her blades bite into their stomachs before the dark crimson spray of Gaarm's blood hit the ground.

Gaarm fell to his knees in agony. Disbelief and pain filled his eyes, and he was now more animal than human. His free hand reached out and grabbed the nearly amputated limb, pushing it against the stump at his elbow, willing it to reattach.

My jaw hung open in a stupid expression of shock, but the show was just beginning. The woman paused as if relishing the sweet move she'd just executed and the intricate engravings lining her bracers glowed with a swirling green light. The energy flowed along her arms and she heaved upwards, lifting both men off their feet and driving her swords deeper into their bodies. My guess is she'd cast some kind of strength spell. With a shout she spun again and flung each impaled man at another of the goons, nearly slicing the impaled men in half.

The last two guys standing must have had a few brain cells rubbing together up top because they backed away. She stood there, waiting, as if she wanted the two men under the corpses of their friends to free themselves before resuming.

"I like to play fair," she said, looking right at me.

Did she read my mind? Where the hell had Gryph found this woman?

It took only a few seconds for two men to become four as the other men heaved their buddies' corpses off of them and rose. They were warier this time and even employed some tactics to their defense.

I'd like to tell you that I got all super heroic and joined the fray, but nope, I froze, mouth hanging open like a slack-jawed yokel. The men moved forward feinting and advancing and for a moment I feared they'd be able to overtake her, and then their rage would turn on me.

Turns out this female death goddess didn't need my help. She knew what these men would do before they did it. It sounds nuts, but she had some kinda *Spidey Sense*. Mustachio parried several blows with his bastard sword as he gained advantage. Now I would have been scared shitless, cuz this dude was skilled. But with every step she took backwards her grin grew wider, more sinister.

He feinted to the left and swung a blow destined to remove her head when suddenly she was a few feet to the left and her right-hand blade had punctured through the side of his neck. I hadn't seen her move, nor, I guess, had Mustachio, since his expression showed more shock than pain as blood sprayed from his mouth.

She pulled her sword free and Mustachio fell in a heap,

twitching as the last bits of life pumped from his ruined neck. The rest of the goons tried to run. Unfortunately for them, she blocked the only way out of the alley, except for the rear door to the inn. They ran towards the door, only to find it locked from the inside. Apparently Master Grimslee had been serious about his distaste for bloodshed in his establishment.

Their eyes blazed panic and one of them begged for his life. A sword through his eye showed that mercy was not forthcoming. Another man bull-rushed her in a flailing whirlwind of desperation that almost found its mark. But again, she seemed to know exactly where he was and she spun low, hamstringing the man. His scream tore at my ears as he fell back onto his ass. She placed the point of her sword on his chest above his heart and smiled down at him.

"You should apologize to my good friend Lex," she said with all the interest of a laborer inspecting the dirt under their fingernail.

"I'm sorry Lex," the man whimpered, fear and agony straining his voice. The woman looked at me and I just stared stupidly back. "Well Lex, he apologized, and I believe he regrets his actions. The polite thing to do is accept his apology."

"Um," I said. "Yeah, like no worries man. We're cool."

A stupid grin of relief crossed the man's face when the woman slowly eased her sword point into his chest. His scream became a bloody sputtering as the sword pierced his heart. I cringed and bile rose in my throat. I leaned to the side to once again empty my stomach when I felt a hand grip my neck.

"Drop your swords now or the priest gets a brain full of steel," said the last man, who'd snuck up on me while his friends were being slaughtered. I felt the cold point of a dagger ease into my ear canal and froze. I raised my hands. "Now buddy, why don't you let me go? This whole thing has nothing to do with me."

"Oh Lex, you couldn't be more wrong," she said. "This has everything to do with you."

"Dammit woman, I'm trying to live here. Can ya keep your damned yapper shut?"

"You've got this Lex. I believe in you," she said, and

leaned on one leg, placing her sword over her shoulder in a far too casual manner for my taste.

"What?" I said stupidly.

"You just need to use your head."

My eyes widened as I caught her meaning. *She can't be serious.* She nodded in a manner that suggested she was reading my thoughts. A plan, a very idiotic plan, formulated in my mind.

"Shut up, both of you. I just want to go home. I didn't even like those guys," the man with the brain skewer said. "Back off and give me your word you won't hurt me, and I'll let him go."

The woman looked at him for a moment and then winked at me. "Nah, don't think so."

"Shit," I said, and the man's arm shook. He knew he was about to die, and I could almost hear the marbles rattling around in his brain as he decided to take me with him.

My mouth had gotten me into this predicament. Maybe she was right; maybe my head could get me out of it. I tensed my legs and leapt upwards with all my might. The blade sliced through the lower part of my earlobe a split second before the top of my head impacted the man's jaw. I felt, or heard, not sure which, bone crack and teeth clatter and the man dropped the dagger. I spun and punched him in the face. He stumbled backwards, falling into a puddle.

I stared down at him and some deep-rooted fury took ahold of me. Before I knew it, my war hammer was in my hands and I'd charged the head with *Spirit* energy. The golden glow seemed almost holy as if I was a scourge of the gods. The man's eyes locked onto mine and I could see that he knew I would kill him. To be fair, I hadn't quite realized that was my intention, but apparently everyone is capable of murderous rage if pushed hard enough.

The man's hand flashed to the hilt of another dagger at his waist and I let go of my hesitation. I brought the hammer down onto his head with a thunderclap of energy. As the sound rolled away and returned as an echo, I looked down on the man's battered corpse. A torso with a massive exploded head that looked like it had been stretched in silly putty. The blink of an incoming prompt broke my stare.

You have earned Experience.

You have earned 875 XP for slaying an Aegyptian Goon.
You have earned 3,256 XP from The Agent's Adventuring Party.

You have reached Level 2.

You have 5 unused Attribute Points.
You have 1 unused Perk Point.

"Cool, experience," I muttered as my rage abated. I shook, as the shock of what I'd just done bit into me. I felt a light hand on my shoulder and looked to see the woman smiling at me.

"Well done," she said.

"There's a bump on my head," I said and felt stupid for it.

"I'm sure kid. But we should go. Only a matter of time before the constables show up, and I've had my fill of killing for tonight."

"You sure?" I said, looking around at the arrayed corpses. She seemed to consider my question, nodded in the affirmative, and then trilled a birdcall so accurate that I almost didn't believe it was coming from her, even while I watched her pursed lips making the sound.

Elves are cool.

From further down the alley three tough looking men emerged from the shadows. Each one looked deadlier than the last. "These are my friends," she said.

"You had pals and did this by yourself?" She gave me a look that asked, 'did it look like I needed help?' I shrugged. "Okay then, now what?" I asked, giving the men a sideways glance. This whole thing was making me nervous.

"We get to the edge of town and then we're out of here," she said.

Two of the silent men took point, and another stepped in behind me. I looked around and my mind went to dark places. Who was this woman? Could I trust her? She turned without another word and walked from the alley. With no other idea of what to do, I followed. We walked in silence. Several homes and buildings had lit candles or lanterns behind barred windows, but nobody seemed curious enough to open them. It seemed townsfolk in the Realms were the same as elsewhere, ignore the sounds of trouble, lock the doors and hope the cops handle it.

Time passed and the *debuffs* I'd accrued from my beating wore off. I felt a lot better as my *Attributes* returned to normal, but the return of my mental faculties came with suspicious thoughts.

"So, where's Gryph?" I asked. There was something that had been bugging me for a while. This Agent was a complete badass, but also a psychotic nutbag. She just didn't seem like the kind of gal that Gryph would send to find me. And why hadn't he come himself?

We reached the edge of town where an arched stone bridge crested a river. I stopped as serious feelings of anxiety crested in me. One man stopped mere inches behind me, invading my personal space. "Dude don't do that." He just stared at me. "Um, what's with Lurch here?"

"He's mute. They're all mute. I find that to be very helpful in my line of work."

"And just what is your line of work?" I asked, as my suspicion grew to apprehension. Something just wasn't right with any of this. She ignored the question and walked across the bridge. The river wasn't wide, but the current was full of eddies and strong swirls.

Lurch stepped in behind me, way too close for comfort. I got the hint and followed the small elf woman. "I don't even know your name."

"Agent works for now. Anonymity is also very helpful in my line of work."

"And what is your line of work?" I asked again.

She stopped in the middle of the bridge and turned on me. "Let's just say I find people who don't want to be found."

I came to an abrupt halt and felt Lurch, well, lurching over me again. The other two took up flanking positions. "Who said I didn't want to be found?" She smiled a grin that would have been arousing if I didn't already know she really, really enjoyed killing people. "Gryph didn't send you," I said.

"No. No he did not," she said, and a small pout crossed her lips as she saw my jaw clench. "I said a friend sent me. I didn't say it was your friend." Hands snatched and held my wrists in an iron grip, and I felt a rope bind them. I struggled but could not budge the massive mute's grip and I knew it was time to panic. Yeah, yeah, I know what you're thinking. What took you so long dude? But, ya gotta cut me some slack. It was my first day of being alive and I was hammered.

I'm sucking at life.

The Agent walked up. "We can do this the easy way or the hard way," she said.

"Wow, kinda cliche, don't ya think? Next thing you're gonna give me a muahahaha laugh."

She cocked her head to the side and gave me a quizzical look. "You're an odd one, you know that? I've never seen a banner NPC with so much personality. Usually you guys are monotone sticks in the mud who take weeks to become interesting. Why are you so different?"

I shrugged my shoulders and gave her a look I imagined was tough. "I'm special. Many people have said so." I immediately felt like an idiot. I wasn't making much of an impression here. It was time to get answers. "What is it you want?"

"Tell me where your Gryph is?"

Of course, she wanted Gryph. She had no real interest in me. See, I'm Gryph's banner NPC, so besides lots of cool benefits, like being his automatic BFF, the gig comes with some pretty cool perks. One being that I can always sense where he is even if he's thousands of miles away.

I'm like a Gryph detector, or maybe a Gryph GPS. There was just one problem, I couldn't feel him, hadn't been able to since I arrived in this crap town. At first, I thought it might be due to whatever *debuffs* Aluran had shocked me with, but after they faded I still couldn't feel him.

"Why do ya wanna know?" I said, in fear and annoyance.

She looked at me and with a flick of her wrist, she suddenly held a thin dirk in her hand. "So, you're choosing the hard way?" She walked up and Lurch held me tighter.

"Hold on, hold on," I said in panic and she stopped a few feet from me. "I don't know where he is, really and truly. I haven't been able to sense him since I arrived here. Why do you think I've been drinking?"

She stared at me for several thunderous heartbeats as if she were trying to extract information from my mind. I panicked for a moment. Was this nut job a *Thought* magician?

The Agent pulled a small glowing stone from her pouch and held it in her palm. "Do you know what this is?"

"A small, glowy pebble," I said, hiding my fear with sarcasm.

She grinned, and I got the sense that she found me amusing. That made me feel warm and fuzzy, but then I remembered she was a psychotic murderer and a chill chased the warmth away. "It's a port stone. A one-time use magic item that will open a portal to anywhere my little heart desires."

"Does your heart desire a nice beach vacation? Margaritas and ceviche maybe?"

She leaned in close to my ear and I felt her warm, sweet breath on my neck. "This is my vacation," she whispered.

I gulped. "Well to each her own I always say."

"Fortunately for you, I'm under orders not to use my more persuasive methods."

She backed away from me, tapping my cheek with the point of her dagger and smiled. "The boss told me I had to bring you to him, even if you told me what I wanted to know."

"Well, wouldn't wanna disappoint the boss."

She turned without another word and walked across the bridge. Lurch pushed me ahead of him and I almost stumbled, but the rope binding my hands jerked me and I realized I was on a leash. "Well this is kinda humiliating. I mean, I like being tied up as much as the next guy, but I'd prefer if Lurch here didn't join the party."

"You got spunk kid," she said over her shoulder. "But, it won't help you when the High God Aluran stares into your soul."

Fuck. A deep panic shot through me. There was no way I'd be able to resist the power of the High God. I couldn't even resist the power of this tiny lunatic and her creepy butlers.

Somehow, I knew that Aluran could get Gryph's location out of me in moments, even if I didn't know where he was. My mind scrambled. A dozen horrible, no good plans rushed through my brain. Each required a skill set or level of badassery that I just didn't possess.

I panicked. I had to do something. Whatever the cost, I could not let Aluran find Gryph. I had to be the hero. Part of my mind hated how loyal I was to Gryph. I mean he was an okay guy, but had he earned the loyalty? A deeper memory almost answered that question when the Agent's amused voice interrupted my thoughts.

"Are you crying?" the Agent asked, and I realized that yes, in fact I was crying.

"No. Maybe." *I'm some hero*, I thought. I stopped and wept some more, just wanting to wallow in my misery.

Lurch was having none of it and pushed me hard. I stumbled and fell onto my face, biting my tongue. The Agent turned and gave Lurch a WTF? look. He shrugged in apology, lifted me up and then pushed me forward again.

"So, if you have this fancy teleportation rock, why do we have to do all this walking?" I asked and spit a wad of blood from my mouth. "Or falling?"

The Agent whipped her thumb back at the town. "See that tower there. It used to be the home of a wizard named Harlan, hence why this town is named Harlan's Watch. He was a bit of a recluse and cast a negation field on the area. Nobody can port in or out. So, we have to get out of the field." She pointed at a hill a few hundred feet from the far side of the bridge.

"That hill marks the end of the negation zone, and incidentally, is where the good folks of Harlan's Watch execute their murderers and rapists. I like that hill."

"Yeah, it's nice," I said. My shoulders slumped in defeat and I walked forward. They say that when you know you're going to die memories of your life flash before your eyes. Well, I'd only been alive a day, so memories of a wonderful life were slim. However, something bubbled up from my subconscious.

A scene from a movie I'd watched a bunch of times back before I'd become buds with Gryph popped into my mind, and I had a plan. It had worked for Rob Roy, so it would work for me. I stumbled intentionally, bringing me closer to the edge of the bridge. Lurch rushed towards me and a bit of slack went into the rope. I leapt up onto the ledge, it wasn't the best leap, but it got me to where I needed to be.

The Agent spun, eyes wide, and yelled "Don't!" Lurch ignored her and reached up to grab me. I looped the rope into a lasso and tossed it over the goon's head. He looked at me in confusion for a moment. Then I jumped off the bridge.

I fell a dozen feet before Lurch's neck arrested my fall, nearly wrenching my arms from their sockets. The giant scrambled at the noose around his neck in panic for a moment before pulling a dagger from the sheathe at his wrist. He sawed at the rope.

"Stop!" I heard the Agent yell in alarm, but she was too late. The rope split and I fell into the rushing water. I cheered inside my head as the current pulled me down stream. *Take that, bitch*, I thought and then I discovered the one, massive flaw in my plan. My hands were still bound, and I had no idea how to swim.

I struggled against the bonds, but they wouldn't budge. Apparently Lurch was more talented with knots than he was with words. I spun and twisted in the current and then sank. My lungs burned, and a prompt popped into my vision.

Debuff Added.
You are drowning. 5 points of damage per second.

Shit, I thought. Then I died.

3

I set my empty mug down onto the table with a hollow thunk, releasing an unexpected spark of energy that made me jump. Gaarm grinned, sucked at some bit of food in his crooked Stonehenge of brown teeth, and pushed his pile of coins forward. "I'm all in," he said.

"What?" I sputtered, my eyes wide in panic. I looked from the coins to Gaarm and back to the coins again. "What?"

"He said all in," The dealer mumbled in a tone that suggested I was an idiot. I sure felt like one. I had no idea what the hell was happening. A moment ago I was drowning. Now I was back in the inn on the cusp of getting my ass kicked.

The dealer snapped his fingers and asked me what I wanted to do? I gave Gaarm a confused grin. "Haven't we done this already?" I asked, looking around the room in panicked confusion.

"We've been doing it for hours dwarf. How drunk are you?"

"I'm an Ordonian," I said in a low, confused voice, and then Gaarm and I said "Really?" at the same time. The large Eldarian's eyes narrowed and his anger rose. "That's what it says," I muttered in a half-hearted manner.

I was alive, and I had no idea why. You see, banner NPC's don't respawn the way Players do. Apparently the developers who hacked the Game Mechanics for Alistair Bechard / Aluran wanted to allow for Player errors, but wanted death to have some meaning, even if the price for that meaning was paid by their NPCs. So, I shouldn't be alive. I'd died and I should have stayed dead.

The pretty barmaid set a fresh pint of Master Grimslee's potent honey mead in front of me. I jumped as the mug thumped the table. I looked up to see her warm smile. We'd done this before too. She smiled at me for a few seconds waiting. All I did was stare like a fool. With a grin that said, 'you're cute when you're drunk,' she reached down and eased one of my coins towards her. "Thanks Seraphine," she said, in a flirty, yet mocking tone.

"Hey, that's my line." I said confused. She gave me the fake smile she'd given hundreds of times to drunken fools like me and slipped the coin into her apron.

"Sir, what do you want to do?" the dealer asked, saying each word very slowly. I looked up at him and his nose scrunched in distaste. The dealer nodded at my card. I looked at it and then up at Gaarm. I knew I had the winning card, but the phantom pain of the beating I'd taken was still fresh in my mind and I had zero desire to make that mistake again. "I fold," I said.

Gaarm smiled and his boys cheered. Part of me hated folding when I had the better hand even if that better hand had come by way of cheating. But, I liked living a lot more, and whatever the hell had just happened was not something I wanted repeated.

"Is everyone else feeling okay?" I asked.

Maybe I was hallucinating. Had Seraphine dosed my mead? I sniffed at my mug. What if she were some kind of assassin? I looked over at her as she brought another mug to the jumpy fire mage. He made a move for her ass, which she deftly blocked and made a no, no, no gesture with her fingers. He stared at her as she skipped away and then saw my eyes on him and held his hand out, sending a brief pulse of flame into the air, as if saying 'that girl's fire.'

"Don't be so sad," Gaarm said to me and I looked at him. "Only way you could have beaten my hand was if you'd cheated. And that would have been a bad idea. I've killed men for less."

"I believe you," I said.

He grinned and slid a coin towards me. "Next drink is on me."

"Thanks," I said, but my mind was already elsewhere. Where was the Agent? If I stayed in here with my new buddy Gaarm, would she leave me be? I knew the answer, and a chill ran through me.

I need to protect Gryph.

34

Wait, what? I'd just died and somehow jumped back in time and was likely facing death again and my first thought was about protecting Gryph. "What is wrong with me?" I mumbled.

"It is called inebriation sir," the dealer said, judging me from on high. I waved my hand dismissively at the man and rubbed at my temples. My head hurt. Not sure if it was cuz I'd died, or cuz I'd come back, or the mead or all of the above. Despite the pain all I could think of was my weird devotion to Gryph. That's when a memory hit me.

Now, for you regular flesh and blood types having a weird memory pop up for no reason is normal. But until today I'd been a ubiquitous quantum matrix with a mind that was much more agile and organized than the squishy grey blob I now carried in my head. Trust me when I say it is a serious downgrade and one I was still getting used to. So it took a few moments to realize the weird images flowing through my brain were memories.

I was in a dim room back on Earth. Holo-vis projectors lined the darkened room and I could feel the hum of numerous quantum cores purring away. My point of view was fixed, and I knew that I was still just a banner AI. *This is the past?*

A scruffy dude in his mid-thirties appeared in my field of vision and I knew I was looking through a camera. This guy seemed familiar somehow, but I couldn't place his name. He looked right at me and smiled.

"Hey, Lex, welcome to the world," the man said and tapped at the virtual keyboard on the desk in front on me. "I'm Sean and you won't remember me later. Sadly, I must block your access to the memories of all these convos until you go into the Realms. I know this is confusing, but you're going to become very special, unique in fact."

"It's ready," said another voice, a strong female voice and then Brynn Caldwell stepped into my frame of view and smiled at me. Now, Brynn I remembered. She'd given me to her brother and started me on this wondrous adventure. Despite all that, I liked Brynn. She handed Sean a pulse drive, an encrypted storage device that used light to store massive amounts of information. He looked at it like it was a holy relic and with a sigh he plugged it into my access port.

"You sure you can do this?" Bryan asked, concern in her voice.

"Pretty sure," Sean said as his hands sped over the virtual keyboard. As he tapped, I felt myself change. I grew … warm, which was odd since I had never felt anything before.

The warmth eased and then another rush of information brought something else, a personality. Why would a banner need a personality? Somehow, I knew this new part of me was ancient. I was about to ask Sean what was happening when the world went black.

Sometime later the world returned. "Is he okay?" Brynn asked. She was staring at me with concern. Sean popped into the frame with an expression of haughty arrogance that only tech nerds seem to be able to pull off. "Pretty sure he's great. Hey buddy, how are you?"

"What am I?" I said and Sean smiled. He gave Brynn an 'I told you so' look and she relaxed.

"Well that is a simple question with a complex answer, but to put it as simply as I can, you are a hybrid entity."

"Hybrid?" I asked.

"Yes, at your base you are a standard issue next generation *Banner*," Sean said proud of himself. "AIs like you will be on the shelves this fall. This new model features a much more complex personality matrix that will allow you to grow and adapt to suit your owner's needs. But, on top of that base and boring bit of tech, you are much more."

"Stop being dramatic," Brynn said, shoving Sean aside. She smiled again. "We sent someone into the Realms to retrieve an ancient artifact called the *Lexicon.* That's what was on the pulse drive you saw."

"The *Lexicon* is an ancient repository of knowledge," Sean said. "Think of it as a Wikipedia for the Realms. We layered it on top of your base code, hence why you're a hybrid entity; part *Banner*, part *Lexicon* and better than both. That's why we call you Lex."

"Clever," I said, with an edge to my tone that I now recognized as sarcasm. This earned a grin of triumph from Sean. "But I'm from the Realms?"

"You used to belong to one of the Old Gods," Brynn

continued.

"Used to?" I asked.

"Yeah, your god is dead," Sean said, earning a glare from Brynn.

"My god is dead?" I asked, and I felt sad. It was an odd emotion no banner had ever experienced.

Sean seemed sad at my reaction. "Yeah, sorry buddy. It's the only way we could make this work. You were Cerrunos' prize possession. If he were still alive, he'd sure notice that we'd stolen you."

"Stolen?" I said, another emotion filling me. Was this anger?

Brynn punched Sean again and looked back at me. "I'd say we freed you. You were trapped in an ancient vault, unused and unloved for millennia. Now we can be friends."

"Friends?" I pondered, and the meaning of the word filled my mind.

"Yes, friends, and we're going to teach you some great stuff and then you're going to be part of a secret mission, a very important secret mission," Brynn said with a smile.

"Secret mission?" I said in a befuddled voice.

"We'll get to that later," Sean said. "Any other questions before we get going?"

"Am I alive?" I asked.

"Good question," Brynn said, but a look crossed her face that suggested she would have preferred nearly any other question. "I'm no philosopher, but, I suspect you'd be able to pass the Turing test, so I'd say yes."

"I'll say maybe," Sean said. Brynn glared at him. "What? You don't know that any more than I do."

Brynn scowled and turned back to me with a smile. "Well, I know one thing, you are very important."

"I think it's time we showed him," Sean said.

"You really think having him watch your collection of stupid movies will help?"

"First, they are not stupid. The movies of the late twentieth and early twenty-first century are classics. Second, there's a lot more than movies in there. I've got TV shows, music, books, classic video games, comic books, the whole gamut. Those stories will help him understand who we are, and why it is important to help keep us safe. Plus, it will occupy him while we finish the integration."

I remembered some of it now. They had me watch, read and play thousands of hours of human entertainment. My AI enabled me to process information much quicker than a human mind could, and I watched Sean's entire collection in just a few days. I learned about love and humor and revenge and loyalty.

That last bit brought another memory to the fore.

"You sure we have to program him for loyalty," Brynn said. "It seems wrong somehow."

"He's isn't human Brynn. I know he seems more like it every day, but he is still a machine, and we need him to do a job."

Brynn looked at me with a sad expression. "You're right."

Then in a flash I was back in the inn. I took a moment to process all that I'd remembered, and then one thought jumped to the fore of my mind. *They programmed me for loyalty.* A scowl crossed my face.

"Fuckers."

"Pardon, sir?" asked the dealer.

I looked up at him. He smiled, looking for all the world like a crane that had decided being a bird was boring and wanted to be a man for a while. I pushed the coin Gaarm had given me towards the irritating man.

"This is for you, for the fine service."

I was certain he picked up on the sarcasm, but he pocketed the coin, anyway. "Thank you kind sir."

I was so lost in my thoughts, fuming and angry thoughts, that I almost didn't notice the door to the inn open. But then my hackles rose, and I sensed eyes on me. I looked up to see the Agent staring at me. Our eyes met and a small smile turned up the corner of her lip. Behind her I could see one of her goons.

At that point I lost all sense of decorum and panicked. I stood so quickly that I jostled the table, sending cards and coins scattering. I heard the dealer complain, but I didn't care. My eyes darted around the room like a terrified rat seeking an escape from a feral cat. She had the front door blocked, and I knew from experience that the back door led to a bottleneck where her other mute goons lurked. I didn't like either option.

Fear punched me in the gut, and I started sweating. *I have to protect Gryph.*

"Dammit, what the hell?" I grumbled in anger. This forced loyalty thing would really put a damper on Gryph's and my relationship.

My eyes scanned the room. I needed help. Gaarm was regaling his buddies with an exaggerated tale about the hand we had literally just played. The pyromaniac mage was setting more stuff on fire at his table before Seraphine tsk tsked him and poured water on his flames. The fat priest was hiccupping into his mead and oblivious.

Even the shadowy rogue's eyes were on the Agent and he seemed tense. I sent a begging stare at him, which he must have felt, cuz his eyes whipped to mine. He simply shook his head no.

"Shit." What was I gonna do? The Agent moved through the crowd towards me as silent as a snake. Nobody seemed to notice her, as she moved in and around people and tables, getting ever closer. My mind screamed, and I had an idea.

"Gaarm," I yelled. "Bounty hunter!" He looked to me and then at the Agent. A guttural growl rumbled from deep within him and he rushed the Agent.

"You won't take me," he said, pulling a dagger.

An odd hush overtook the room as every eye in the place went to the Agent and Gaarm. She smiled and drew one of her swords. He stabbed, and she parried the blow with ease, backing away to let his momentum take him past. She smacked the flat of her blade against the back of his thighs, earning a grunt.

I took advantage of the distraction and dove to the floor, scuttling under tables and past legs, hoping I was heading in the general direction of the front door. Hopefully Gaarm could distract her enough for me to reach the door and then disappear. I know what you're thinking, real brave man, crawling away from a tiny elf girl, but I am a survivor above all else.

I crawled and dodged the panicked feet of people scattering to give the combatants room. Several people tripped over me, a few stepped on my hands, and one kicked me in the face. I got so turned around that I ended up by the front window. I risked a look and realized my position was no better. Both Gaarm and the Agent were between the door and me.

Steel rang against steel as Gaarm and the Agent battled. I knew that she could have easily killed him. Why wasn't she? Maybe she didn't want to murder someone with so many witnesses? It was just as likely that she enjoyed teasing Gaarm. After all she was a self-admitted sadist.

"You ain't taking me alive," Gaarm yelled, and dove towards the Agent once again.

A sudden twang split the air, followed quickly by the thunk of a crossbow bolt sinking into a support beam a few inches from Gaarm. The noise silenced everyone, and all eyes turned towards the bar.

"Cut that shit out, both of you," said a deep voice I recognized as Master Grimslee's. I peeked up to see he was reloading his crossbow.

"I ain't goin' with her," Gaarm said in way of explanation, eyes never leaving the Agent.

"Don't care what you do. Just do it outside," Grimslee said.

At least the man was consistent. Grimslee finished loading the crossbow and leveled it at the Agent. "Think about your next action very carefully lassie."

With a fluid motion, the Agent sheathed her sword and smiled at Grimslee. "I don't want trouble. I've just come for my quarry and then I'll go."

"Already said I ain't goin' with ya," Gaarm said.

"I'm not here for you," she said.

"Huh?" he muttered, and his shoulders relaxed. "No?"

"No. I'm here for him," and she pointed at my hiding spot. Most of the patrons couldn't see me crouched behind the chair. "Stand up kid. I know you're there."

I slowly stood, my hands raised like a perp in some stupid cop show and tried to hold eye contact. Grimslee turned his crossbow on me.

"You should go with the nice lady," he said.

"What?" I sputtered. "Somebody just walks into your place of business, harasses one of your customers and you're okay with that?"

I could almost see the indecision swirling in Grimslee's mind when the Agent pulled an official looking piece of parchment from her bag and showed it to the innkeeper.

"This is an official Warrant of Summons that gives me the authority to take this man, known as Lex, to the Capital City of Avernia to face charges of murder, sedition, treason and heresy."

Everyone in the inn's common room backed away from me. A haze flashed through Grimslee's eyes and he aimed his crossbow at me.

"Well shit," I said.

"Get out of my inn."

Everyone in the common room stood down as the Agent slunk her way towards me. I backed up in a panic, but there was nowhere to go. *I must protect Gryph.*

"Dammit, shut up." I looked around, panic gripping me. I didn't want to·jump off that damned bridge again. Drowning is a crappy way to go.

I felt a light breeze against the back of my neck and turned to see a half open window. An idea came to me and I turned back to the Agent. Her eyes went wide as if she knew what I was intending and increased her pace. I ran a few steps towards her and then turned back towards the window. With a grunt I sprinted towards the window and jumped through.

Well, not exactly through. You know how in movies, action heroes routinely jump through windows, do a badass tuck and roll and then get back to their feet amidst a shower of diamond like glass? Yeah, that is not how it happened for me. I went through the window all right, but the window did not shatter in a glorious rain of sparkling jewels.

No, that is not what happened at all. Some of the glass broke and some of it didn't. Knife like shards bit into my face and shoulders as my momentum carried me through. The wood of the window frame snagged my legs, and I fell forward, face planting onto the ground outside the window.

You are Severely Bleeding. 5 DMG/Sec.
You are Concussed.
Intelligence and Dexterity reduced by 5 for 30 minutes.

"Ouch," I said and spat out a mouthful of dirt as glass continued to tinkle down around me. A shard of wood had stabbed through my calf, trapping my leg. I was in agony and nearly upside down. I panicked and pulled hard, shooting terrible pain through my leg. My *Health* was dropping fast.

Inside the inn I could hear yelling and laughter. Above all was Grimslee's angry baritone. I looked back towards the window to see the Agent pull the curtains aside. She smiled down at me as I struggled to free my leg. On instinct I fired an *Order Bolt*. It hit her and did less than a tickle from Elmo.

"What the hell?"

"You've made this so much more fun," she grinned. I wrenched my leg again, this time pulling it free with an agonizing tear. I fell to the ground and crab walked backwards. The Agent flicked the few remaining spears of glass and wood from the window with a casual backhand. She then leaped through the window with the grace of a cat and landed lightly on her feet.

"That's what I was trying to do," I said as I stumbled to my feet. She smiled at me, advancing slowly. I was in bad shape, but I would not give up without a fight. I pulled my war hammer from the holster on my back and got into my best fighting stance.

The Agent grinned again and slowly eased her two swords from the sheaths at her back. "I promise I won't hurt you, she said. I just want to talk."

"Oh yeah, I know. Your Eminence the High God just wants to talk." I really wanted to make air quotes, but the heavy hammer in my hands made that impossible. The Agent's eyes became slits, and I smiled. At least I'd earned that small victory. I knew more than she did. But it was fleeting, as all jest left her face and she advanced on me.

I panicked and ran. Well, ran may be generous, it was

more of a drunken, crippled hobble. I moved as fast as I could and felt the adrenaline ease the pain. I was getting closer to a major cross street where a large crowd was going about their evening business. Maybe, just maybe I could hide among them.

I risked a look behind me to see the Agent was still not running. I would have fired another useless *Order Bolt*, but my stupid cooldown clock was still ticking down. I turned back to the road and as I crossed, I heard a whiny and a yell of "Whoa!" and had just enough time to see the flaring nostrils of a large horse pulling a cart laden with stone, bearing down on me.

"Shit," I said as the horse barreled into me, followed quickly by the heavy cart. As my bones snapped and my organs burst I saw the Agent look down on me with a genuine look of anger.

Then I was dead, again.

4

I set my empty mug down onto the table with a hollow thunk, releasing an unexpected spark of energy that made me jump. Gaarm grinned, sucked at some bit of food in his crooked Stonehenge of brown teeth, and pushed his pile of coins forward. "I'm all in," he said.

"Ahhhgghhh!" I yelled at the top of my lungs and my hands quickly patted down my body. No cart tracks or crushed organs or splintered bones. I was whole, in body if not mind. "What the hell is going on?"

Gaarm and the other players jumped at my outburst, but the dealer simply stared down on me, a look of calm disdain on his face. "You are inebriated sir," he said.

I looked up at him, panic and the phantom terror of being crushed to death still very much with me. "Ahhhgghhh!" I screamed again.

"Shut your yapper dwarf," Gaarm said in an irritated voice.

"I'm an Ordonian," I said in a voice brought low by shock.

"Really?" Gaarm said.

"That's what it says," I said, again. This line of conversation was getting old. What the hell was going on? This was the third time I'd lived this same moment, and I'd died twice. It's like I was stuck in a time loop. Realization made my eyes go wide. "Oh, shit, I'm in Groundhog's Day," I said.

"Whatchoo yammering 'bout?" Gaarm grumbled.

"Groundhog's Day, 1993, starring Bill Murray and Andie MacDowell. Directed by Harold Ramis." Gaarm just gave me a blank stare. "Great movie." Gaarm stared some more.

"Sir, the gentleman has gone all in. What do you want to do?"

My eyes snapped to the door, looking for the Agent. "Too soon," I mumbled, cursing myself for not remembering

44

exactly when she'd shown up. I stood and tossed my card face up on the pile of coins. Anger burned into the large Eldarian's face. "I fold," I said.

"Are you sure sir? You have the winning hand."

"Yeah, I'm sure. I cheated. Feel really bad about that. What's say I buy you a drink? Some of the good stuff as an apology."

Gaarm looked ready to stand and grab me as he had before when he realized I'd folded. Finally, he gave me a confused nod. He looked at the dealer who simply shrugged and then Gaarm dragged the pile of coin towards him.

I took my focus away from the angry felon and kept my eyes on the door. Panic and uncertainty built in me. I needed to find a different tactic.

Jumping through the window had been painful and ineffective.

I eyeballed the back door and considered making a run for it, but I knew at least two of the Agent's minions were hiding that way. I realized I was sick of running. It was time to go on the offensive.

So, I hid behind a planter near the door and waited. Time moved like a slug through salt as I waited, and I kept getting eyeballed by people for my odd behavior. Even the twitchy fire mage was giving me a judgmental stare.

Great, I'm the resident weirdo.

Finally, the Agent entered, and I jumped from my hiding space and fired *Order Bolt*. The spell's description said it "will unerringly hit" its target. Guess what, it did, but the energy flowed off her like oil fleeing Dawn dish soap in that damn commercial.

The Agent has resisted Order Magic.
Better luck next time.

"Shit, even the prompts are becoming assholes," I said, and tried to run. Soon I was at the bridge again. I tried to let her take me. After my traumatic past few lives I really would have been okay with not dying. But that damn loyalty reared its ugly head again and the next thing I knew I was drowning.

I think I hate you Gryph, I thought and immediately felt guilty. *Bastard.*

I was back at the table and this time I only kinda squealed like a preteen girl. Gaarm looked at me in irritation, repeated his dwarf insult, and the ever-smug dealer asked me what I wished to do. I folded again. Gaarm gave me the stink eye, his tiny brain debating whether he should kill me for not really cheating. I was shaking. My nerves were shot. I'd died several times already, and I had no idea how to stop it from happening again.

"Hey Gaarm, ol' buddy, I could use a stiff drink. You want one?" I felt the stare of his too close-set eyes burning into me before he nodded and grunted. "I'll take that as a yes," I said and walked up to the bar.

Master Grimslee was polishing mugs with his favorite snot rag and I put on my best winning smile. "My friend and I feel like celebrating," I said, tossing a thumb over my shoulder at Gaarm.

"Good for you," Grimslee grumbled, eyes staring at me levelly.

I glanced back at the door. Still no Agent. I turned back to Grimslee. "Now, I know you must have some finer stock, perhaps hidden out back?"

"You don't like my mead?"

"No, no, I love it, but I just felt like something with more punch, something a tad pricier, perhaps. My friend and I are celebrating."

"You said that already," the innkeeper said, but he glanced at Gaarm who pointed at himself with a nod. "Well, okay then. I got some elvish brandy and some Eldarian fire wine."

I pretended to consider for a moment. "Whichever one is the most expensive, and the most hidden out back." Master

Grimslee gave me an odd look, but then grunted and tossed his rag onto the bar. He pushed the curtain to the back room aside and disappeared.

"And pour yourself one while you're at it," I yelled after him. A grunt that almost sounded pleased came from behind the curtain. I gave it a second and then rushed behind the bar. "It's around here somewhere," I said in a low voice. The first shelf held a bunch of mugs. The second bits and odds and ends. Finally, on the bottom shelf I saw it, the butt of a loaded crossbow.

I grabbed the weapon and eased it onto the bar. It was a fine weapon and its weight felt good in my hands. I placed the weapon on the bar top, removed the safety catch and took aim at the door. I inhaled deeply, trying to calm my pounding heart.

The shadow laden rogue's eyes locked onto mine, but he neither moved nor said a word. As his cigarillo lit up the inside of his hood, I could see a small smile. Seraphine sauntered up and plopped a few empty mugs onto the bar. She looked at me with casual calm. "Whatcha doin' hun?"

"Target practice," I said and returned all my focus to the door as the handle twisted and the door eased open. A second later I saw the Agent. She looked about the room and I took aim. I pulled the trigger and the twang of the drawn string sent the bolt flying towards the Agent. I knew right away that my aim was true.

The bolt flew right towards the small elf woman and a mere second before it hit her she took a step back. The bolt flew by and sunk into the neck of the fat priest. His look of shock was only slightly greater than my own. He slumped forward, dumping his mug of mead down his cassock. The Agent's eyes came to mine, and she smiled.

"What the hell?" I said. Nobody moves that fast. It's like she knew the attack was coming. My eyes went wide. "Spidey sense."

You have earned Experience.
You have earned 923 XP for slaying a Priest of Ferrancia.

Sorry dude. But killing the hapless priest gave me a new skill.

You have learned the skill ARCHERY.

Level: 1.
Tier: Base.
Skill Type: Active.

You have shown that you can handle bows and crossbows. This ability will allow you to deal death from a distance.

Base Chance To Hit is one's Dexterity +1% per level. Chance of Critical Hit = 1% per level.

You have reached Level 3.

You have 10 unused Attribute Points. (5 New and 5 Previously Earned)
You have 2 unused Perk Point. (1 New and 1 Previously Earned)

I didn't have time to play with my points just yet and swiped the prompts away in annoyance. I tossed the crossbow down and ran towards the back door. The Agent and one of her mutes followed. Now, I'd like to tell you that I got away, but, yeah, that didn't happen. I ran headlong into her other goons and I ended up tied up at the edge of town again.

Damn loyalty. I made a promise to myself, that if I ever saw Gryph again, I'd punch him in the face. Then I jumped off the bridge. I didn't even fight it this time; I just let the water take me.

And I died, again.

I set my empty mug down onto the table with a hollow thunk, releasing an unexpected spark of energy that made me jump. Gaarm grinned, sucked at some bit of food in his crooked Stonehenge of brown teeth, and pushed his pile of coins forward.

"I'm all in," he said.

Blah, blah, I cheated, etcetera, ad infinitum. I won't bore you with all this again. Now that I realized I was stuck in some kinda weird time loop, I had to figure out why and then figure out how to get unstuck.

I was a bit calmer this time and cast *Commune* again. Knowing my luck, the bastard Lords of Order would claim that since I was technically reliving the same day, I wouldn't be able to can the spell again. But happy day, the world went hazy and up floated a quadrata. I had no clue if this was the same one that I'd spoken to before, but I still felt that he, she, it, should have a name. I named it after the world's most famous cube.

"Hey Rubik, how's it hangin'?" The quadrata just stared at me with an unnerving, unblinking eye. "Right, my question? Can you tell me where Gryph is?"

NO, it thought said and floated away.

"Dammit," I mumbled as the world returned.

Okay, I still needed to fight my way out of this. My mind ran through the possibilities and I decided the crossbow was still my best option. But this time, I'd hide behind the bar, until I heard the Agent and her crony enter. Then using the mirror behind the bar that Master Grimslee never seemed to clean, I'd wait until she was facing away from me. Then I'd spring up and fire. No chance she'd avoid that.

Well, guess what, she avoided it. But at least I got my first Critical Hit, with a brutally lucky shot to her minion's eye.

You have earned Experience.

You have earned 1,523 XP for slaying an Agent's Thrall.

Thrall? Were these guys slaves? Under some kinda mind control? Who was this chick?

She turned and grinned at me. I dropped the crossbow and ran to the back door again. I knew where the other thralls were hiding, so I was sure I could avoid them. I was lucky with the first one. He was hidden well back from the alley, so he couldn't see me until I was almost on top of him. I slunk along the far wall, hidden in shadows.

You have learned the skill STEALTH.

Level: 1.
Tier: Base.
Skill Type: Active.

You have shown that you can be sneaky and stealthy. This ability will allow you to hide from enemies, sneak up on them to use the Pickpocket skill or to perform a sneak attack.

Base Stealth success percentage is determined by Dexterity +1% per level of Stealth.

Right as I was sneaking by thrall #2 the back door to the inn opened and the Agent looked right at me. Apparently, my *Stealth* skill still sucked. I jumped up and sprinted past thrall #3. He made a grab for me, but I slipped under his grasp. Guess being short for an Ordonian had some benefits. I ran towards the end of the alley.

Damn these stumpy legs.

I did some quick calculations in my mind. I'm great with calculations. Remember, I was an artificial intelligence in a past life. If I was right, then this plan would work. My lungs burned with the effort and I promised myself that regardless what happened next, some good old-fashioned cardio was in my future.

I could hear the thrall right behind me and I put on a last, desperate burst of speed. As I crossed the road, I heard a surprised whiny and a "Whoa." My calculations had been correct.

To my left I saw the flaring nostrils of the horse that had trampled me the last time. It whinnied again, and the driver tried to pull up. But, stopping several tons of horse and cart proved impossible, again, and the thrall behind me was crushed to a pulp. I nearly threw up at the sight. The once man looked like a sack full of organs and bone dropped from an incredible height. And the blood, there was a lot of blood.

Is that what I had looked like? Damn.

I pulled my eyes away from the carnage and ran again. But my *Stamina* was crap, and it wasn't long before the Agent and her last thrall had me again. They tied me up, the Agent blathered and at the bridge I jumped.

This time I wanted to make it quick. I exhaled violently, forcing all the air from my lungs with a terrible underwater laugh. Trust me that is harder to do than one thinks. The subconscious mind tends to defeat the conscious when survival is at stake, but my subconscious mind had never faced such intense and obvious stupidity as purposely drowning myself. I think I caught it by surprise.

I drowned and died, again.

5

I was back where I'd started, again.

I got a *YES* from Rubik when I asked if I was stuck in a time loop. So, I'm not insane. Yay me.

I took careful aim with the crossbow and fired. The Agent dodged again. The thrall did not.

You have earned Experience.

You have earned 1,523 XP for slaying the Agent's Thrall.

I ran. They caught me. It was the same old, same old. This time I added some flair to my dive from the bridge. I'm sure it would have at least won me the bronze.

And, then I was back again. I moved to a different spot and took careful aim. The bolt zipped at the Agent and she stepped aside. This time I hit the barmaid, and I got a *Critical Hit*.

You have earned Experience.

You have earned 2,153 XP for slaying Seraphine.

I felt bad about that one.

> ### You have reached Level 4.
>
> *You have 15 unused Attribute Points. (5 New and 10 Previously Earned)*
> *You have 3 unused Perk Point. (1 New and 2 Previously Earned)*

I stared at the prompt for a moment and realized that I was keeping my experience after each death. I know it seems obvious to you, but I was so stressed out about dying repeatedly, that I had kinda glossed over it. I was leveling.

I had another chat with Rubik. "Hey, my multi-faceted friend how's the family?" As usual, I got nothing. With a heavy sigh, I asked my question. "Can I beat the Agent?"

NO, it said and floated away.

"Dammit," I said, and I sank into a real depression. Maybe that's why I let the Agent take me this time. If I was gonna die, then I may at least productively use my last few moments. It was time to spend some points.

Order Bolt was cool, but it didn't do squat to the Agent, and it would be a while before *Mana* would become a problem there.

My god Cerrunos was dead, so I didn't have any incantations. That shitty situation convinced me that I needed to up my physical *Attributes*.

My *Stamina* had gotten me killed several times already, so I dumped 5 points into *Constitution*. I put another 5 into *Dexterity*, thinking that maybe it would help my aim, or at the very least my ability to escape capture. I dumped my last 5 points into *Strength*, cuz ya know, 'smash smash, crush head' with my war hammer would be much more effective.

Lex - Level 4	Stats
Ordonian Deity: Cerrunos Experience: 10,253 Next Level: 4.747	Health: 140 Stamina: 144 Mana: 145 Spirit: 145
Attributes	**Gifts**
Strength: 23 Constitution: 19 Dexterity: 17 Intelligence: 16 Wisdom: 16	Player Tracking (Gryph) Ordonian Bloodlust Attribute Points: 0 Perk Points: 3

The surge of warmth and power that flowed through me, almost made me forget about my imminent death. Then I felt Lurch tie my hands, and the Agent chirped up.

"Tell me where Gryph is?"

This again.

"I told you already, I don't know," I said.

"Told me? When?" she said, giving me a strange look.

"Oh, right, that was the last time."

Her eyes narrowed in suspicion and with a flick of her wrist, she suddenly held a thin dirk in her hand. "Explain that statement?" She walked up and Lurch held me a bit tighter.

"Nah, I don't want to. Let's just do what we do," I said.

She tapped the dagger against my cheek. "You're an odd one. I like that."

"So, you'll let me go?"

"Sorry. No can do," she said, flipped her dagger back into its sheath and pulled the port stone from her pouch.

"Ooh, the pretty rock. And yeah, I know you love the Hill of Death at the edge of town."

The look she gave me sent a chill into my bones. Had my charming love of sarcasm led me to say too much? She clearly had some kind of prognostication capability, some way of knowing the future or sensing danger. How else had she avoided my attempts to kill her every damn time?

"Shit," I said and ran to the edge of the bridge. She moved too quickly, and I could not properly lasso Lurch this time. He reached for me as I plummeted over the edge of the bridge and the rope tangled around his right arm. He made the mistake of trying to arrest my fall and as the rope jerked, I heard Lurch grunt in pain as his arm snapped. I fared no better as the sudden jerk, mixed with the odd angle I was falling, wrenched both my shoulders from their sockets. I screamed in agony as my body spun, dangling from the rope like an unspooled yoyo.

I don't know if it was the pain, the uselessness of his broken arm, the weight of my body, or all three, but the rope went slack, and Lurch pitched over the side of the bridge. We both fell into the water and I screamed in joy as the water rushed into my throat and lungs.

This time I made a Molotov cocktail out of Master Grimslee's rotgut liquor. Of course, I didn't hit the Agent with either the improvised grenade or the crossbow. The Molotov exploded on the fire mage who grinned in some horrid combination of pain and ecstasy as he burst into flames. *That guy has issues.* The crossbow bolt took the thrall in the neck again. Yay, another *Critical Hit* for Lex.

You have earned Experience.

You have earned 1,223 XP for slaying a Fire Mage.

You have earned 1,523 XP for slaying the Agent's Thrall.

I continued to cast *Commune.* "Hey Rubik, will I ever be capable of beating the Agent?"

YES, it said and floated away.

"Well, yay," I said as the world returned and the Agent caught up with me. I smiled up at her with renewed confidence. "Your days are numbered bitch." I was almost happy to drown this time.

I fired the crossbow a bunch more, sometimes killing the thrall, sometimes sending a random bystander into the next life, but never once coming close to scratching the Agent.

I tried to hire the twitchy fire mage to attack her as soon as she walked through the door. But he wasn't interested, and I spent so much time arguing with the weirdo that the Agent was there before I knew it. Then things went pretty much as normal for me.

I tried the Agent as a bounty hunter trick on Gaarm a few times. As I ran the screams of Gaarm and his cronies bit into me with a stab of guilt. I got a bit further those times, but, not far enough.

There were a bunch of other things I tried.

"Dammit."

"Ouch."

"Crap."

"Really? Now that is just messed up."

So, yeah, I kept dying, which was getting really old. On the bright side, I was earning a butt load of XPs, upped my skills a bunch and even earned a few more levels.

You have earned Experience.
You have earned 7,338 XP for slaying a Fire Mage (x6).
You have earned 4,615 XP for slaying a Priest of Ferrancia (x5)
You have earned 22,845 XP for slaying the Agent's Thrall (x15)
You have earned 21,530 XP for slaying Seraphine. (X10)

I felt a bit bad for killing Seraphine so many times, but since she was reborn anyway I quickly got over the feeling. I took a while to notice just how much XP killing her gave me.

Earning that many XP for killing a simple barmaid made no sense. There was more to sweet Seraphine than met the eye. I made a promise to myself that I would uncover her secrets as soon as I was able.

My Q & A sessions with Rubik became increasingly frustrating. Once I asked if it knew how I could defeat the Agent and it thought *YES*. But, knowing how and being able to tell me how with just a *YES* or *NO* answer was another matter. When I asked it directly if it could tell me how to defeat her it said *NO*. The cubic idiot knew how I could win but could not tell me how.

I wasn't getting anywhere fast, and that made me angry.

So, I took it out on Gaarm. Killing him didn't help me escape the Agent, but I really hated that guy. So, I killed him a bunch and got some good experience.

You have earned Experience.

You have earned 9,920 XP for slaying Gaarm (x5)

And I gained a new skill after evading Gaarm's clumsy dagger attack.

You have learned the skill DODGE.

Level: 1.
Tier: Base.
Skill Type: Active.

You have showed proficiency in Dodge. Dodge allows the user to avoid an attack, thus incurring no damage. Chance to Dodge is a percentage chance based on the user's Dexterity +1% per level in Dodge - the opponent's level in the skill used to attack. Heavy armor wearers suffer a penalty to Dodge.

Just for shits and giggles I even tried to shoot the shifty rogue who was a big fan of smoking and looking mysterious. Every time he evaded my attack. His skill differed from the Agent's ability. He was looking right at me, so I gathered he had a very high *Dodge* skill. She moved aside without knowing I was there. Her Spidey Sense was way cooler than my *Dodge* skill.

You have reached Level 5, 6, 7, 8, and 9.

You have 25 unused Attribute Points.
You have 8 unused Perk Point. (5 New and 3 Previously Earned)

Your Skills have Levelled.

You have reached Level 10 in Order Magic.

You have reached Level 8 in Archery.

You have reached Level 8 in Blunt Weapons.

You have reached Level 4 in Stealth.

You have reached Level 1 in Dodge.

You have reached Level 6 in Light Armor.

You have reached Level 15 in Analyze.

Casting *Commune* and *Order Blast* was upping my *Order Magic* skill slowly, but steadily. I'd never planned to use my *Archery* skill, but its constant leveling made me wonder if I should rethink that. After all, who didn't love playing the sneaky archer?

Apparently, my constant people watching had seriously upped my *Analyze* skill. It gave me an idea. I needed more information if I was ever to extract myself from this hellacious time loop. It was time to spend some *Perk Points*. I opened my *Analyze Perk Tree*.

Analyze Perk Tree.			
Tier	Understanding	Defense	Learn
Base	Detect Falsehood	Block Analyze	Skill Resistance 1
Apprentice	Know Desires	False Report 1	Skill Resistance 2
Journeyman	Know Falsehoods	False Report 2	Spell Osmosis
Master	Know Skills	False Report 3	Skill Osmosis
Grandmaster	Know Perks	False Report 4	Perk Osmosis

Analyze Perk Tree Understanding.

----- Understanding -----

Those who invest in the Understanding branch of the Analyze Perk Tree can glean important information from an opponent. All Understanding Perks require that the user's Analyze skill be of a higher level than the opponent or creature to be effective.

Detect Falsehoods.

This perk enables the user to detect whether an Analyzed person or creature is lying, hiding a truth or being evasive. The nature of the lie will remain a mystery.

Know Desires.

This perk enables the user to know what an Analyzed person or creature wants. Every person and creature craves understanding.

The Know Falsehoods.

This perk enables the user to not only Detect Falsehoods, but to know what the lie concerns. This can uncover deep, dark secrets.

Know Skill.

This perk enables a user to see what skills a person or creature possesses. It also enables the user to know what level the person or creature possesses in that skill up to the level of the user's Analyze skill.

Know Perks.

This perk enables a user to see what perks a person or creature possesses.

Analyze Perk Tree Defense.

----- Defense -----

Those who invest in the Defense branch of the Analyze Perk Tree can defend their own information from an opponent. All Defense Perks require that the user's Analyze skill be of a higher level than the opponent or creature to be effective.

Block Analyze.

This perk enables a user to block a person or opponent's own Analyze skill. If the user of this perk is of a higher level than the opponent, then the opponent's Analyze attempt will fail.

False Report 1.

This perk enables the user to present a false Strength when Analyzed.

False Report 2.

This perk enables the user to present a false Immunity when Analyzed. Users are also immune to others use of False Report 1.

The False Report 3.

This perk enables the user to present a false Weakness when Analyzed. Users are also immune to others use of False Report 2.

The False Report 4.

This perk enables the user to present a false set of Skills (and their levels) and a false set of Perks when Analyzed. Users are also immune to other's use of False Report 3.

Note: False Reports must be set up in advance and can be changed at will.

Analyze Perk Tree Learn.

----- Learn -----

Those who invest in the Learn branch of the Analyze Perk Tree can learn how to defend themselves from the Skills and Perks of an opponent. At higher tiers the user can learn Skills and Perks from an opponent. All Learn Perks require that the user's Analyze skill be of a higher level than the opponent or creature to be effective.

Skill Resistance 1.

This perk enables the user to reduce the effectiveness of any one skill used by an opponent by 25% for the duration of the encounter. After the encounter is over the 'immunity' disappears.

Skill Resistance 2.

This perk enables the user to reduce the effectiveness of any one skill used by an opponent by 50% for the duration of the encounter. After the encounter is over the 'immunity' disappears.

Spell Osmosis.

This perk enables the user to Analyze and learn a spell that is cast by a person or creature. To learn the spell, the user must have an Affinity for that sphere. Requires that the user already possess the requisite magic skill. The user can only absorb the knowledge of the spell if they already have gained that Tier in the magic skill. This perk can only be used once per week. Success of Spell Osmosis is determined as (Intelligence/2 + Analyze Level /2) - (Opponent's Intelligence/3 + Opponent's Analyze/3).

Skill Osmosis.

This perk enables a user to Analyze and learn a skill that is being actively used by a person or creature. The learned skill will always be Level 1 regardless of the level possessed by the Analyzed person or creature. This perk can only be used once per week. The user must have a higher Analyze skill than the opponents own Analyze skill and the user's Analyze skill level must also be of a higher level than the opponent's level in the skill being learned. (Requires Know Skills Perk). Success of Skill Osmosis is determined as (Intelligence/3 + Analyze Level /3) - (Opponent's Intelligence/4 + Opponent's Analyze/4).

Perk Osmosis.

This perk enables a user to Analyze and learn a perk that is being actively used by a person or creature. The user will also learn the associated skill if they do not already possess that skill. The learned perk must be of a tier capable of being learned by the user. The user must have a higher Analyze skill than the opponents own Analyze skill and the user's Analyze skill level must also be of a higher level than the opponent's level in the skill being learned. This perk can only be used once per month. (Requires Know Perks Perk). Success of Perk Osmosis is determined as (Intelligence/4 + Analyze Level /4) - (Opponent's Intelligence/5 + Opponent's Analyze/5).

"Sweet," I said. The _Analyze_ perks would be my ticket out.

"Should I assume that means you wish to go all in sir?" the dealer asked.

I motioned with a dismissive hand that I was folding. "I don't have time for your pompous attitude Jeeves," I said. "I got me some spending to do."

My eyes lingered on the _Learn_ branch. Without hesitation I put a point into _Skill Resistance 1_. The perk may not help me overcome the Agent on its lonesome, but I sure wouldn't sneeze at the idea of reducing the effectiveness of one of the Agent's skills by 25%. What I was really after were the higher _Tier Perks_.

I was currently level 15 in _Analyze,_ which meant I had a way to go before I could purchase the truly great perks like _Osmosis._ But, if I had one thing on my side it was time. I reread the descriptions several times as my plan solidified. I dumped another point into both _Detect Falsehoods_ and _Block Analyze._ I had no idea if they'd be effective against the Agent, but every bit helped, right?

I was so engrossed in my task that I did not see the Agent enter until she tapped me on the shoulder. I jumped a bit and looked up. This time, when the Agent took me, I smiled at her.

During our nice walk to the bridge I dumped 25 _Attribute Points_ into _Intelligence._ It was a bold move putting all those points in one basket, but if I would ever get out of this damned time loop, it would be due to brains not brawn, and _Analyze_ thrived on _Intelligence._ Plus, if the plan brewing in my brain worked, I'd soon refill that well.

6

I was back where it all started. I folded, gave Seraphine a much larger tip than normal and swigged my mug of mead down in one gulp. A satisfied burp erupted from my innards, then I stood and raised my war hammer over my head. I had a plan.

"Time to grind."

I poured *Spirit* into the war hammer and brought it down with terrific force onto Gaarm's head. The idiotic look on his face as he realized what was about to happen was a gift I would have paid to see with several lives. In fact, I had done exactly that. The hammer crushed his skull amidst a flash of golden light. Brains and bits of skull exploded in a wide circle and an odd silence settled for the briefest of moments.

Then the screaming started, I swung my hammer down onto the dealer's head. Now, technically that wasn't the nicest thing to do, but he was an intensely irritating human.

You have earned Experience.
You have earned 1,984 XP for slaying Gaarm.
You have earned 462 XP for slaying the Dealer.

I got in a few more blows before Grimslee's crossbow bolt took me in the neck.

I did a bunch more grinding, both of my *Order Magic* and my *Blunt Weapons* skill. Using my *Ordonian Bloodlust* gift helped me get a bit further down my list of "People to Kill." Each time I ended up dead, either from Grimslee's crossbow or Gaarm's buddies overwhelming numbers, or if I was a bit tired and didn't feel like grinding, the good old-fashioned drown in the river method.

Once, after Rubik gave a particularly irritating non-answer, I even tried to send the quadrata into the next life, assuming it had one. That didn't go so well. My hammer bounced off it and then it fired some kinda *Order Magic* death beam from its eye and burned me to a crisp. I even got a prompt about that.

ATTENTION.

Attacking servants of the Lords of Order in the Realm of Order is unwise. On their home plane their powers are multiplied by a factor of 10 while yours are reduced by a factor of 10.

"Good to know." The cool thing was, the next time I had a chat with Rubik it didn't seem to remember my previous faux pa. It even gave a satisfactory *NO* when I asked it if it was angry with me. Rubik was a nice cube.

I decided that it was time for a well-deserved vacation. Wanton murder was hard work, and I needed to relax and do some shopping. I opened my prompts.

You have earned Experience.

You have earned 79,360 XP for slaying Gaarm (x40)

You have earned 9,240 XP for slaying the Dealer (x20)

You have earned 18,975 XP for slaying Mustachio (x15)

You have earned 17,265 XP for slaying Aegyptian Goon (x15)

You have earned 91,610 XP for slaying Gaarm's Goon(s) (x80)

You have earned 29,352 XP for slaying a Fire Mage (x20)

"Holy Shit!" I said and looked across the table at Gaarm. "Gaarm ol' buddy, I think I may be a bit unstable."

"I don't care dwarf, just call or fold," Gaarm muttered.

"I'm Ordonian," I said with a smile. "Beware my bloodlust." Gaarm just stared at me and I tossed my card onto the table. "Fine, I fold," I said and returned to my prompts.

Lex - Level 14	Stats
Ordonian Deity: Cerrunos Experience: 474,489 Next Level: 25,753	Health: 174 Stamina: 182 Mana: 199 Spirit: 174
Attributes	**Gifts**
Strength: 23 Constitution: 19 Dexterity: 17 Intelligence: 41 Wisdom: 16	Player Detection Ordonian Bloodlust Attribute Points: 25 Perk Points: 10

You have reached Apprentice Tier in Analyze.

With that Tier boost, the skill has gained a new ability. You can now see the Strength(s) of anyone successfully Analyzed.

I was both amazed, and irritated, at my skill progression. Thrilled, cuz duh, look at me I was becoming a total badass, and I'd advanced to the *Apprentice Tier* in *Analyze*. Irritated because I was one level away from the *Apprentice Tier* in *Order Magic*. What kinda goodies would the next *Tier* open?

"I'm pretty sure somebody is messing with me."

"No sir, you are just inebriated. There is no messing," the dealer said, the last part with such disdain that I have no idea how Jeeves didn't pull a muscle.

Now you know why I only felt mild qualms about killing the pompous fool. He was a dick. I gave him a small grumble as I considered my next move. It was time to spend some more points. I quickly put 15 points into *Intelligence*. I wanted more *Mana*. The other 10, I put into *Constitution*. If I was to survive, I needed to up my *Health*. Part of me realized how lucky I was, from a certain point of view. Other beings in the

Realms would never have had the grinding opportunities I've had. Course they also had a little something called freedom. I kept my *Perk Points* in reserve until my plan was better formulated.

I'd lost track of how many times I'd lived and died. Had I been in this loop for weeks, months, decades? I had no clue. Apparently going all nut job and killing random people without consequence can skew one's sense of reality. Once, as I stood in a room full of corpses covered in blood, I even had a crisis of conscious.

"I may be going a bit psycho."

But, I had a solid estimate for the time from my rebirth until the Agent's appearance at the door. It averaged 10 to 15 minutes. Various factors, including how active I was, whether I left the inn or stayed and the level of chaos inside the inn, seemed to alter this. But, until my evidence was more solid I'd assume I had 10 minutes of me time in each life.

It was time to change my strategy from mass murder to the kinder and gentler idea of learning about my fellow inn-mates. Maybe, in learning about them, I could gain allies, skills or weapons. I smacked my head in a duh moment. Why hadn't I tried to loot any of my innumerable victims? I guessed that I wouldn't be able to take the swag back in time, but you don't know until you try.

It was time to use my new ability, so I *Analyzed* Gaarm.

Gaarm.
Level: 8 *Health:* 183. *Stamina:* 197. *Mana:* 112. *Spirit:* 123.
Gaarm is an Eldarian.
Strengths: Mark of Vex. *Immunities:* Unknown. *Weaknesses:* Unknown

I focused on the phrase *Mark of Vex*.

Mark of Vex.

The Vex is an Eldarian criminal syndicate with tendrils all across the planet of Korynn. It is a power player in the criminal underworld.

The Mark of Vex is a magical tattoo that not only identifies the owner as a member of the organization but also grants a +1 bonus to Strength, Constitution and Dexterity as long as the bearer remains loyal to the organization.

"Well, well, well, Gaarm, you're a made man." The large Eldarian just stared at me in confusion, bordering on anger. Seraphine brought me another mug of mead, but I told her to give it to Gaarm instead. The gesture seemed to allay his suspicions, and he returned his attention to his pals.

I opened my *Analyze Perk Tree* and dumped points into *Know Desires, False Report 1* and *Skill Resistance 2*. Maybe now I'd be able to see what that Agent bitch wanted. And if not, I could lie to her and show her I was, say, a badass in ninjutsu, when I wasn't. Okay, dumb example, but I always wanted to be Sho Kusogi. While potentially less fun, *Skill Resistance 2* could be the key to my maybe surviving the Agent next time.

It was time to test out my new perks. I activated *Know Desires*. "Hey Gaarm, old buddy, old pal, why exactly are you a wanted man?"

"Cuz' I kill pip-squeak dwarves like you who ask stupid questions," Gaarm said, leaning forward in his chair with a murderous scowl.

"I'm Ordonian..." I said when a prompt window interrupted my words.

You have successfully used Know Desires on Gaarm.

Your Analyze level combined with your Intelligence was too much for his small mind to resist. You not only know that Gaarm is lying, but you also know what he truly desires. Gaarm has an unhealthy appetite for sexual relations with livestock.

Wow, my first quest. I looked up at Gaarm. "Bestiality? Really Gaarm? Lay off the livestock buddy."

The Eldarian coughed up some of his mead as anger and shock surged into his eyes. He pulled his dagger and jumped across the table at me, aiming to skewer my throat. I activated *Dodge* and his blade missed its mark, but still made a glancing blow against my robes. My *Health* bar dipped by about 10%, which annoyed me more than hurt me. I stood, powered up my hammer and crushed the idiot's head.

You have earned Experience.

You have earned 1,984 XP for slaying Gaarm.

Screams filled the room, and I shrugged. Guess my evolution to a kindler, gender Lex would have to wait. I swung my hammer in lazy arcs, not really caring who I killed or how many. I took some shots of my own and my *Health* bar ticked downwards.

You have earned Experience.

You have earned 462 XP for slaying the Dealer.

You have earned 1,265 XP for slaying Mustachio.

You have earned 1,151 XP for slaying Aegyptian Goon.

After a minute of this another well-aimed crossbow bolt split my Adam's apple. *Nice shot*, I thought and fell to the ground, blood flowing from my ruined throat.

I died.

7

I was back, again. It was time to enact Plan 2.0, Make Friends. I scanned the room and my eyes fell to the twitchy fire mage. I know what you're thinking, that guy is a nut job. Yes, he is, but he also knew magic and maybe, just maybe, he would teach me. I needed to understand the weird pyro, so I *Analyzed* him with *Know Falsehood*s.

Arno Malik.

Level: 9.
Health: 178
Stamina: 163.
Mana: 175.
Spirit: 124
Race: Aegyptian

Arno Malik is the seventh son of a minor noble family from Gypt.

Strengths: +20% Fire Damage.
Immunities: Unknown.
Weaknesses: Unknown.

You have successfully used Know Desires on Arno Malik.

Your Analyze level combined with your Intelligence was too much for his unstable mind to resist.

You now know that Arno just wants love and forgiveness. He wants to belong after his obsessive love of fire caused the accidental death of his entire family.

Bounty for the Pyromaniac.

Arno Malik of Gypt, is wanted for questioning in the matter of the death of his entire family in a mysterious fire. Turn him into the proper authorities.

<u>Difficulty</u>: *Moderate.*
<u>Reward</u>: *100 gold pieces.*
<u>Experience</u>: *5,000*

No wonder the dude is so twitchy. I felt bad for him, and unlike Gaarm, had no desire to turn him in. But, at the moment I couldn't let sentiment get the better of me. Arno had skills that I needed.

I chatted the guy up over several lifetimes and eventually learned what he wanted. He didn't want money. He didn't care that I threatened to tell the constable about him. He didn't even want a date with Seraphine. Like I said the guy was weird. I finally realized that what he wanted was a friend, a comrade-in-arms, someone to make him feel less psycho and alone.

"So, the deal is, I teach you *Fire Magic*," he said, eyes glowing with an internal fire. "And then we burn this place to the ground with everyone in it?"

"Yup," I said and that little voice deep inside chirped up again. *Nice job staying away from going psycho dude.* "Shut up," I said.

"Excuse me?" Arno asked, his eyes squinting in suspicion.

"Nothing let's burn this joint," I said with a cheery thumbs up.

Arno jumped to his feet with such excitement that he almost knocked Seraphine over. She gave him an irritated look, but then went on her way. Arno stared after her.

"Sure, you don't want to let her live?" I asked. He shook his head no and gave me a creepy leer. "Well, okay then," I said, and Arno placed his hands on my head. A raging inferno leapt up my arms and into my mind.

You have learned the spell Flames.

Sphere: Fire Magic.
Tier: Base.

Allows the caster to fire a continuous stream of fire from their hand. Base Damage: 10 (+1 per five levels of Fire Magic). Does an additional 5 pts. (+1 per five levels of Fire Magic) of damage every second that Flames is active.

Mana Cost: 20 + 20 Pts./Sec.
Duration: Until cancelled or Mana runs out.
Cooldown: None

You have learned the skill FIRE MAGIC.

Level: 1.
Tier: Base.
Skill Type: Active.

You can now wield the power of Fire Magic. Fire Magic allows the user to manipulate fire and heat. Fire magic is primarily an offensive magic, but it also has some defensive spells and can be used to summon creatures made of fire. Fire mages are notoriously hot tempered, often unstable and considered very dangerous.

Well, that description has got you pegged Arno my pal. Flames was a pretty cool spell, but also very basic. I asked Arno if he had any other spells he could teach me.

"No," he said, a perplexed look crossing his face. "Why would anyone need one?"

"Okay then," I said. "Let's get burning." Arno grinned, and I got a prompt.

You have been invited to join Arno's **Adventuring Party**.

Already knowing that I would regret it I hit **ACCEPT**.

The bonuses were sweet though the fact that they were tied to my dedication to pyromania was a bit unnerving. I should have known the crazy was about to get much worse.

Arno looked back at me with a grin and then thrust both hands out. Jets of flame erupted from his palms. The heat and power were incredible, and a sheen of sweat covered my skin. Arno pulsed his flames over all the people in the inn and the screams of agony and the smell of charred flesh made me gag.

What have I done?

Sure, I'd murdered nearly everyone in this building more times than I could count, but there was something truly terrifying about fire. I couldn't take it and I pointed my palms at Arno and unleashed fiery hell. His eyes darted back to me with that same look of agony and ecstasy I'd seen on him where I'd killed him with the Molotov cocktail. The lunatic had never been happier.

Arno died.

You have earned Experience.

You have earned 1,223 XP for slaying Arno
You have earned 26,235 XP from Arno's Adventuring Party.

The flames were consuming every surface in the room and I knew there was no way I was getting out. I knew dying by fire would be pure agony, so I did the only thing I could think of. I took huge breaths. Better to die by smoke inhalation than by fire. I collapsed to the ground as the smoke stole my breath and noted, with no small amount of annoyance, that Arno had done what I could not. The shifty rogue with the cigarillo was a charred corpse, still sitting in his chair.

I died.

I spent the next several lives learning about the other inn-mates in my prison of time. Gaarm had no interest in helping me with anything, and his bullying kept all his goons in line. The dealer was useless, as his one power seemed to be pretentiousness.

For the price of a mug of mead, and a willingness to listen to him blather on and on about his belief that everyone in town was a chthonic demon worshipper, I convinced Percinius, the Priest of Ferrancia to teach me *Life Magic*. That dude had a serious dislike of demons.

You have learned the spell Minor Healing.

Sphere: Life Magic.
Tier: Base.

You can now heal minor wounds on yourself and others. Heals 20 points of Damage (+ 2 per level of Life Magic)

Mana Cost: 20.
Casting Time: 2 seconds.
Duration: N/A.
Cooldown: 30 seconds

You have learned the skill LIFE MAGIC.

Level: 1.
Tier: Base.
Skill Type: Active

You are now able to wield the power of Life Magic. Life Magic allows the user to tap into the animating forces of life and sentience itself. Life Magic primarily makes use of defensive and healing spells, but also has some potent offensive spells.

Note: *Users of Life Magic are beloved for their abilities to heal, to enable crops to grow quicker and to make life better.*

Next, I turned my attentions to Seraphine. I'd known that something wasn't quite on the level with her for a while. Her XP payout should have been somewhere in the range of Jeeves the dealer's 462, but it was over four times higher. I used *Analyze* and *Know Desires* on her.

Analyze has failed.

Know Desires has failed.

Seraphine's eyes locked on mine and the deep grey that I'd previously thought was beautiful became sinister. She advanced on me, slipping a wickedly sharp dagger from her apron.

"Well damn," I said and powered up my war hammer. She got in a surprising number of strikes before I took her down. When she was finally dead, I knelt at her corpse.

You have earned Experience.

You have earned 2,153 XP for slaying Seraphine.

Debuff Added.

You are Severely Bleeding.
5 Dmg/Sec until your wound is staunched.

Debuff Added.

You have been Poisoned.
5 Dmg/Sec for 10 seconds.

Knowing I didn't have much time, I searched her. I found

a small vial of black liquid that gave me the creeps and a rolled-up scroll of parchment. I tried to open the parchment, but no matter how much I tugged, tore and pulled the ribbon would not come free.

You have found a Secure Scroll.

Designed to protect secrets, Secure Scrolls will only reveal their secrets with the utterance of the correct password or phrase.

"Crap," I grumbled through gritted teeth. "Stupid scroll." A crossbow bolt hit me in the back and my *Health* bar blinked alarmingly. I shook the parchment in annoyance and then had a thought. I cast *Commune*.

The world paused and as the mists rolled in my pain subsided. *That's an interesting side effect*. A moment later Rubik floated up. Now, I had no clue if this idea would work, but ever since reading the *Commune* description, I'd been wondering exactly what a *Boon* was, but I suspected one could help me now. I knew one thing, my question needed to be precise to get a *Boon* from the ever-vague floating box.

"Will you tell me the password or phrase to open this scroll?" I asked and held the rolled parchment up in front of Rubik's never blinking eye. It stared at me for several heartbeats and I felt like a child digging for the prize at the bottom of a cereal box, desperate for it to be something great, but fearing it would be a cheap hunk of crap.

YES, it thought at me and I felt rubbery fingers grab my head. It was a bit disconcerting being mere inches from an unblinking eye the size of a dinner plate. But then a tingle ran through my body, similar to the restructuring sensation I'd felt when I'd learned *Commune*. Then, a single word popped into my brain.

Daffodil.

Rubik removed its hands, but instead of floating away it hovered there for a moment, its unblinking eye looking me up and down. I felt like a hot chick being ogled by construction workers.

"What's up pal?" I asked, as a sense of worry flowed through me. Its pupil dilated and a rubbery hand whipped out, grabbing my belt and pulling me close. "Hey!" I yelled in alarm, and scenes of creepy inter-planar molestation rushed through my head. "I'm not that kinda guy," I said, and then Rubik dug into my satchel and removed my *Writs of Cerrunos*. "Hey, that's mine." It just stared at me. "Right, *Boons* require a payment. Go ahead, it's not like I'm using it, anyway. Stupid dead god." Then I remembered it would end up back in my satchel when my next life started anyway, so no harm no foul.

The cubic creature held the book in both hands and then a slit appeared beneath the large eye. The slit parted to reveal a mouth full of sharp, symmetrical teeth. I backed up a bit and then with no ceremony the quadrata crammed the book into its mouth, its teeth tearing at it like a paper shredder. Rubik finished his papery meal, turned and floated away.

"Well okay then," I said, puzzled. "At least I got a *Boon*," I said and did a.little jump in triumph. Then doubt settled into my heart. "Wait, daffodil? Are you sure?" I called after Rubik, knowing I would get no answer. The mists faded, time moved forwards again and pain tore into my body, and I was back dying over Seraphine's body. I heard yelling and the sound of many feet rushing my way and knew I only had seconds left.

"Daffodil," I said. The ribbon around the scroll glowed and untied itself. The scroll unfurled and suddenly I knew what it contained.

Contract.

Subject: This scroll is a bound contract between the Assassin known as Seraphine and the Vex.

Target: Master Grimslee, Owner and Operator of the Shining Unicorn Inn and the local leader of the Durnarian Syndicate.

Payment: 1,000 gold.

"Oh, Master Grimslee, you're like the Godfather." I looked up at the grim-faced innkeeper as he took aim with his crossbow. "You picked the wrong side pal," I said and laughed. The twang of the crossbow announced the end of that life.

My next life had a single mission, discover what the creepy liquid Seraphine carried was all about. This time I didn't even bother killing her, I just groped my way into her apron and stole it. I know, it was kinda pervo stalker behavior, and I felt bad about that. Is it odd that my groping made me feel worse than all the murder?

Seraphine's eyes widened in alarm as I pulled the small stopper from the vial and downed the black liquid like a bro chugging Jaeger. For a moment nothing happened. Seraphine just stared at me with wide eyes.

I grinned at her and a single word popped into my brain. "Daffodil," I said. Her eyes widened in panic and then my gut churned in agony.

Now, I'd died a whole bunch of times and some of them were incredibly painful, but that little vial of poison was so horrid I still shiver thinking about it.

The liquid melted my flesh. It started with my lips and then bubbled into my mouth and down my throat. My teeth melted, and a hole appeared in my throat. I coughed up blood as the poison boiled away my flesh.

Debuff Added.

You have been Poisoned.

You have been poisoned by the Bane of Life, an acidic poison that is melting your body.

Bane of Life is immune to Counter Agents and renders Healing Spells and Potions ineffective for 10 seconds.

50 damage per second for 10 seconds.

You bitch, I thought. I would have said it, but my throat and mouth had burned away, and I could no longer speak.

Then, thankfully, I died.

I may have freaked out a bit when I came back from that death. I could still feel the phantom pain of my flesh melting, so I walked up to Seraphine and unloaded my full *Mana* pool into *Order Bolt*. My assault looked like a burst of pure white fireworks unloading into her face. The energy surged into her body.

At level 19 in *Order Magic*, I could fire three bolts per casting, each doing eight points of damage. Due to my level I had only a one second cooldown, so she had little ability to recover between my castings. With 199 *Mana* I could fire the spell nine times before running out. That was a whopping 216 points of damage.

My *Mana* dried up, and with it came a massive headache, like a migraine delivered by a spike of ice to my temple. I bent over, gritting my teeth in pain, and was stunned to see Seraphine stumble to her feet. Dammit, this girl was tough. I powered up my hammer with *Spirit* energy and took a home run swing. She collapsed in a heap.

You have earned Experience.
You have earned 2,153 XP for slaying Seraphine.

A stunned silence filled the inn as I looked around, mad eyes begging anyone to say something. Gaarm laughed, answering a question that had bugged me for some time. Despite their common connection to the Vex, it seemed he and Seraphine were not working together. I gave the brute a thumbs up.

I turned back to Seraphine's corpse and heard the scrape of a dozen chairs as most of the patrons in the Shining Unicorn Inn quickly exited. How long did I have before the constables showed up?

I reached down and pulled the *Secure Scroll* from Seraphine's apron and walked to the bar. Master Grimslee had his crossbow aimed at me but did not fire. Perhaps he didn't believe he could take me out after I went all nut job on his waitress. I looked from the scroll to Grimslee.

You have been offered the Choice Quest.

Meddle in the Gang War

Seraphine is an assassin hired by the Vex to kill Master Grimslee, innkeeper and local mob boss for the Durnarian Syndicate. You have proof of this in the form of a Secure Scroll contract. Now you have a choice to make.

A) You can warn Master Grimslee and earn the ire of both Seraphine and the Vex.
Difficulty: Moderate.
Reward: Unknown.
Experience: Unknown.

B) You can keep quiet and let Seraphine do her work.
Difficulty: Moderate.
Reward: Unknown.
Experience: Unknown.

C) You can turn one, or both, in to the proper authorities, assuming those proper authorities are not on the take. Who to trust, who to trust?
Difficulty: Moderate.
Reward: Unknown.
Experience: Unknown.

Oooh, it's like a Choose your Own Adventure book, but I can't cheat and look ahead. I considered for a few moments and then tossed the scroll onto the bar top.

"She was here to kill you. Password is Daffodil," I said. His eyes went from me to the scroll and back to me as I walked past him and into the back room. I grabbed a fresh bottle of elvish brandy and returned to the common room. I poured two snifters full of the liquor and pushed one towards Grimslee. "You're gonna need it." I lifted my own snifter and admired the pale-yellow liquid before inhaling and taking a sip. Grimslee stood beside me reading the scroll. His face went pale, and he looked at me. "How did you know?"

"Her and I go way back," I said and downed my drink. "You should thank me. That poison is a bitch."

"Thank you. I owe you a favor," Grimslee said.

"I'll hold you to that," I said, and poured another brandy. I held my snifter up in a toast. After a moment Grimslee did the same. The clink of glasses brought a prompt into my vision.

You have completed a Quest.

You have been awarded 10,000 XP for completing the Choice Quest **Meddle in the Gang War.**

You have saved Master Grimslee from the deadly assassin Seraphine.

You have earned a Favor from Master Grimslee.

You have earned the Ire of the Vex. The Vex have eyes everywhere and knowledge of your actions will soon get back to them. You will soon have a contract on your head.

Well, I guess no bad deed goes unpunished. Soon I'd have a bounty on my head. I turned towards Gaarm and his buddies, wondering which one was the 'eyes' mentioned in the prompt. I could have killed them all, but I kinda liked the idea of having my own Wanted poster. Hopefully they'd get my likeness right. Then I remembered this whole timeline would never exist for them, and I got a little pouty. It felt good being notorious.

I decided I needed a breather, so I sat next to Arno. The twitchy mage grinned at me and opened his mouth. "Not, now bud," I said, cutting the pyromaniac off before he could speak. I'd leveled again, and I wanted to spend my last few minutes of this life shopping.

"Sweet," I said.

The Agent walked into the inn and came to say hi.

"Damn, you're early," I said, without even looking up. "I still have points to spend." She tensed, and I felt the energy of imminent action pulse through her. I looked up and stared directly into her eyes. "Maybe it's for the best. I'll have some extra time to plan." Her eyes turned to slits as she tried to understand my cocky attitude.

I stood and leaned towards her, very much invading her personal space. "This is the last time I play nice," I said, and then I turned and walked towards the door.

After a few paces I turned back. "You coming?"

8

I was back in the inn with an empty mug and a happy grin. I tossed my card down, told the dealer I folded and leaned back in my chair. Seraphine brought me another mug of mead and even though, or perhaps because, I'd just gone batshit crazy on the assassin I felt generous and pushed my entire pile of coins at her. Then I stood.

I was getting close to beating the Agent, I could feel it in my bones. There was only one more person I hadn't spoken too yet, and I had an odd feeling he would be very helpful. I looked at the rogue in the corner. This dude was an enigma. I'd never once killed him and *Analyze* had failed every time. Maybe it was time to chat up the dude.

I made my way through the crowd, counting down the minutes before the Agent appeared. I stopped in front of the rogue and tried *Analyze* just for the hell of it.

Analyze has failed.

"Eh, worth a try," I muttered. "May I?" I asked indicating the empty chair. The rogue nodded, and I sat. "I don't have time to waste, so I'll get right to it. Who are you and what makes you so special?"

The rogue grinned, stubbed out his cigarillo and leaned forward. "Took you long enough to come and say hi."

"What?" I said in genuine shock. Did this dude know I was in a time loop? Was he somehow responsible? I stood and old habits caused me to power up my hammer with *Spirit* energy before I knew what I had done.

"Relax. I'm a friend and I have a proposal for you."

Reluctantly I powered down the hammer. I didn't trust the

dude, but my murderous ways had given me a bit of an itchy trigger finger, and sometimes I hit before I thought. I was trying to change that. You know, trying to grow as a person.

I used my *Know Desires* perk.

Know Desires had failed.

"Yeah, that won't work either. Not unless I allow it. Though I have to say, nice job with your *Analyze* skill. Do you know how hard it is to level that skill? I took decades to get where you are. How long have you been working on it?"

"Just a day," I said with bravado.

"Okay, then." He said with a bemused grin and motioned to my seat. "Sit and I'll allow you to *Analyze* me."

I eyeballed the guy a few moments before taking a seat. That was a new one. I had no idea that you could allow somebody full access with *Analyze*. Either the guy was crazy, stupid, or he knew he had nothing to fear from me.

My heart beat in my chest for several seconds as I contemplated his words. It felt odd being on the defensive again. I'd spent so long as the aggressor with the upper hand, except against the Agent of course, that this new reality was unnerving. *Maybe I should go back to mass murder.*

"Okay, I get you have no reason to trust me. Here's an olive branch," The rogue said. He closed his eyes and looked inward. Professional pride that I hadn't ever been able to kill him mixed with my unease, and I considered smashing in his head with my hammer. But a little voice chirped up from deep inside me. *Dude stop being a psycho.* I grumbled but did as the voice asked. A moment later the rogue opened his eyes and smiled.

"Try now. I'm an open book."

I used *Analyze*.

Vonn Sennig.
Level: 37. _Health_: 465. _Stamina_: 435. _Mana_: 434. _Spirit_: 767. _Race_: Half Elf (Eldarian/Sea Elf). _Specialty_: Templar of the Source. _Vonn Sennig is a Templar of the Source, a religious knight by way of a rogue, whose mission is to recruit the NPC Lex to serve a higher power and a higher purpose._

"Um, what?" I said, looking up at the shadow shrouded man in surprise. I had innumerable questions and not much time to get answers. By my count, the Agent would walk through the door at any moment.

"I'm Vonn Sennig," the rogue said, extending a hand towards me. "And I'm here to help."

"Are you in a time loop too?" I asked and immediately felt dumb. I'd just given super-secret info to a man that for all I know was playing me. Sure, he let me _Analyze_ him, but how did I know he hadn't maxed out the _Defense_ branch of the _Analyze Perk Tree_. That trick he'd just pulled sounded exactly like something one could do with _False Report_.

"Is that what it is?" Vonn asked. "I knew something was off. I've been getting impressions of things, echoes, but I had no idea it was a time loop."

"Can you help me get out of it?"

"Don't think so. That's not my purpose. But who knows, maybe my purpose will help you with yours."

"Are you always so cryptic?"

"Lately, yes I have been."

For a moment I just stared at him. Seraphine stopped by and dropped a mug of mead in front of me and a snifter of elvish brandy. I looked down at my mug and up at Seraphine. "Can you bring me what he's having?" She smiled and walked back to the bar.

"You have questions," Vonn said.

"Ya think? How do you know things about me? What the hell is the Source? What is a Templar? What is a Specialty? How do you know who I am? Why am I your mission? And what the heck is a higher purpose?"

"That's a lot of questions. Do we have the time for me to answer them all?"

I eyeballed him again and sent a quick glance to the door. This dude's knowledge was creeping me out. I needed a second opinion. I cast *Commune,* and the world stopped as the mists rolled in. My quadrata pal Rubik floated up and stared.

"Hey buddy, can I trust Vonn?"

YES, came the immediate reply, and the cube floated away. Time began again. Vonn was looking around, a slight frown of confusion on his face.

"Well, that was weird," the half elf muttered, shaking his head as if he were clearing cobwebs.

"What was weird?" I asked, panic surging once again.

"It was like a blip. One second you were here and then you weren't and then, blip, you were back again."

"Okay, now I'm getting annoyed. Time to answer my questions."

"Yes, of course. Where to start? Well, I am a Templar of the Source, a sort of religious warrior. Though my skill set is less knight in shining armor than it is shifty rogue, but my dedication and faith are as strong as any paladin's. Long ago I was called to the service of the Source and the Source has sent me here to help you."

"The Source? I've heard that term somewhere before. What is it?"

"It is everything." Vonn said and quickly held a hand up at my irritation. "But, I understand that is not very helpful. The Source is the truth of the Realms, the motive power behind all of reality. It has always been and always will be and is the source of all. It tries to guide all mortals towards a better existence."

"You're talking about God," I said. *Great, he's a religious wacko. Just what I need.*

"Yes, but not a god with a small g like the petty tyrants and power brokers currently worshipped on Korynn. The so-called Pantheon."

"Are you some kinda Jim Jones wanna be?"

"I have no idea who that is, but to answer the question behind the question, no I am no cult leader who demands devotion. I am here to free your mind and draw it to the higher purpose of the Source."

"What purpose?"

"To help all sentient beings across all the Realms find their true purpose."

"That sounds great, if vague and redundant. How does the Source plan to do that?"

Vonn shrugged. "I only know my small part. The Source is far too vast for any mortal mind to fathom."

I held a hand to my head. This circular talk was hurting my brain. "Okay," I said through closed eyes. "Did the Source do this to me? And if so why?"

"I cannot say. I am not privy to the Source's plan. But, I can help you."

"How?"

Vonn's help came in the form of training, lots and lots of training. We started with *Dodge and Light Armor*. *Dodge* training involved Vonn stabbing me while I tried to avoid his attack. If I did, my *Dodge* improved. If I didn't, my *Light Armor* got a few ticks better. It was a very painful, yet effective method. After many stabby deaths I got pretty good at it.

Your Skills have Levelled.

You have reached Level 16 in Dodge.

You have reached Level 17 in Light Armor.

We only had 15 minutes each training session, and I my *Light Armor* and *Dodge* skills continued to improve. That meant I was back to jumping off the bridge frequently. But that was okay since I kept my promise to the Agent about no longer playing nice. I used *Order Bolt* to kill her thralls over and over and hit her a bunch of times too, but she still resisted.

You have earned Experience.

You have earned 68,535 XP for slaying the Agent's Thrall (x45).

Your Skills have Levelled.

You have reached Level 21 in Order Magic.

"Man is that it?" It was getting harder and harder to level these skills. Don't get me wrong it made sense. I understood the *Game Mechanics* were designed for balance, but it didn't mean I wasn't gonna whine about it. That's when a thought occurred to me.

"Yo Vonn, did the Source create the *Game Mechanics*?"

"The Source is the *Game Mechanics*," he replied flatly, and looked at me like an asshole college professor.

We played some more, and I died some more. Vonn gave me tips on how to up my *Stealth* skill a ton by playing hide and seek with the other inn-mates. I got pretty good at it too and used it to get some sweet *Critical Hits* on Gaarm. Those made me smile like a nerdy girl asked to the prom by the school hunk. I leveled *Blunt Weapons* a few times since that was my *Stealth* attack of choice. I even upped *Light Armor* by a level when my *Stealth* attempts failed.

You have earned Experience.

You have earned 79,360 XP for slaying Gaarm (x40)

Your Skills have Levelled.

You have reached Level 18 in Blunt Weapons.

You have reached Level 16 in Stealth.

You have reached Level 18 in Light Armor.

I saw that Vonn was a master at *Pickpocket* as well and made him teach me. Once again Gaarm was my focus, but Seraphine had some snazzy stuff too, so I robbed her plenty.

Not that I got to keep it when I came back. Remember that loot theory? Yeah it proved to be true, cuz I didn't get to keep anything in my next life. My *Pickpocket* training didn't work out so well at first and I got caught a lot which forced me to go all murdery again and again.

You have learned the skill PICKPOCKET.

Level: 1.
Tier: Base.
Skill Type: Active

You have shown that you have deft fingers and a love for other people's belongings. This ability will allow you to pilfer belongings from innocent bystanders without being caught. Base Pickpocket success percentage is determined by starting Dexterity +1% per Pickpocket Level. High Analyze and Perception skills will negate this ability.

You have earned Experience.

You have earned 19,840 XP for slaying Gaarm (x10)

You have earned 2,310 XP for slaying the Dealer (x5)

You have earned 6,325 XP for slaying Mustachio (x5)

You have earned 5,755 XP for slaying Aegyptian Goon (x5)

You have earned 5,725 XP for slaying Gaarm's Goon(s) (x10)

You have earned Experience.
You have earned 7,338 XP for slaying Arno the Fire Mage (x5)
You have earned 4,615 XP for slaying a Priest of Ferrancia (x5)
You have earned 21,530 XP for slaying Seraphine. (X10)
You have earned 24,550 XP for slaying Master Grimslee (x10)

All the grinding earned me another level, and bumps in my skills.

You have reached Level 15.
You have 5 unused Attribute Points.
You have 8 unused Perk Point. (1 New and 7 Previously Earned)

Your Skills have Levelled.
You have reached Level 5 in Life Magic.
You have reached Level 6 in Fire Magic.
You have reached Level 19 in Blunt Weapons.
You have reached Level 18 in Stealth.
You have reached Level 17 in Dodge.
You have reached Level 19 in Light Armor.
You have reached Level 25 in Analyze.
You have reached Level 6 in Pickpocket.

I only had 5 *Attribute Points*, but they went into *Constitution* with all the hesitation of a nerd getting a pic with a cosplay chick at Comic-Con.

I was going to need more *Stamina* very soon.

Lex - Level 15	Stats
Ordonian Deity: Cerrunos Experience: 767,000 Next Level: 123,000	Health: 180 Stamina: 195 Mana: 221 Spirit: 177
Attributes	**Gifts**
Strength: 23 Constitution: 34 Dexterity: 17 Intelligence: 55 Wisdom: 16	Player Tracking (Gryph) Ordonian Bloodlust Attribute Points: 0 Perk Points: 8

I told Vonn I wanted to spend some *Perk Points*. They were adding up and burning a hole in my britches like a paperboy's summer earnings. But, like a conservative dad, Vonn convinced me to wait and see where my skill set took me.

I even got to know Vonn a bit too. Apart from the frequent stabbings, he was a pretty stand-up guy. Truth be told, he was my only friend in the Realms. Gryph had abandoned me. My god was dead. I think I just needed a sympathetic ear. He even told me a bit of his story. Perhaps that was why I gave his crazy religion a chance.

"I was in a bad way," Vonn said. "There were bounties on my head and obligations to some very bad people that I knew I could not keep. I was a dead man walking in the strictest sense of the phrase. The worst thing was, I knew it to be true. I was desperate and alone, and one day as I left the pub where I liked to drown my sorrows, I was murdered."

"Wait, wait, wait, what?" I said, leaning forward and sloshing some of the fine Eldarian fire wine onto the table. "Hold on, are you a Player?"

"No."

"But you were murdered, and we're talking?"

"The Source," Vonn said simply, hands held wide. "I

cannot explain it any other way."

How potent is this shit? I thought and eyeballed the glass of brandy I held at a very precarious angle as I sought evidence of foul play. Seraphine was an assassin after all, maybe she dosed me with something less acidic and more hallucinogenic.

"We'll continue this next time," he said.

That's when the Agent tapped me on the shoulder. With a sigh, I went for a walk, killed a thrall with *Order Bolt*, jumped off the bridge and died.

Vonn and I had a few more speed dates and then, abruptly, he told me our time was up. I was devastated, like when football season ends or that cute and quirky girl on *The Bachelor* doesn't get a rose. He stood and walked towards the door. As he got close, he turned back to me.

"Do you remember the first time we met?" he asked.

"Um, yeah, it was right here," I said pointing at the table that would always be our table.

"Wrong," he said with a grin. "How do you think you came by that extremely rare spell stone?"

My mind flashed back to the beginning of the day. I was lying in the dust after Aluran's energy Tourette's had jacked me up, with a half dozen villagers looking down upon me. Amidst that sea of missing teeth and crossed eyes, was Vonn. In my memory he smiled and snapped an 'atta boy' at me, but I'm pretty sure that was a fiction created by my need.

"You gave me the *Commune* stone," I said in awe as the memory broke.

"I do as the Source bids," he said, and turned towards the door. He pushed it open and stopped. He glanced back at me. "It is the gift that keeps on giving."

"Will I see you again?" I asked, and immediately felt desperate, alone and stupid. I'd see the dude in a few minutes, when this fuck-all loop began again.

"If the Source wills," he said and turned away. He held the door open for someone who turned out to be the Agent.

What a gentleman? I thought. *What a prick*?

I felt alone and confused. I'd become so used to the complete freedom of my actions having no consequences that I think I may have lost my humanity. But my actions had consequences, perhaps not for the endlessly reborn people that shared my world, but for me, for my mind, perhaps even for my soul. Assuming a one-time AI even had a soul.

These thoughts filled my mind as the Agent arrived. I was so lost in my own world of regret that I let the Agent take me to the bridge without complaint. A few times I mumbled "Uh huh," or "Yeah," to the questions the Agent asked me. My mind was absent, and when I saw the bridge, I ran and dove off.

Death was a relief.

☠☠☠☠☠

I was back at the table across from Gaarm. I looked across the room to Vonn's spot. He wasn't there. A knot twisted at the center of my stomach, a combination of fear and desperate sadness. My only friend had gone. How? Why?

"Sir, the gentleman has called," the dealer said in his nasally voice. .

"I fold," I said in a small voice and just sat there staring at Vonn's empty seat. I have no idea how long I sat there when Gaarm kicked my chair under the table.

"Hey dwarf, what's the matter with you?"

I jumped and stared at the Eldarian. "I'm Ordonian," I muttered. Like a flash inspiration came in the form of Vonn's voice.

I knew what needed to be done. Everything I'd been through since I'd first landed flat on my ass in that dusty street had been leading to this. It had all been part of some grand plan, a crazy conspiracy. Vonn's words trilled through my mind.

"It is the gift that keeps on giving."

Yeah, yeah, you were expecting 'If the Source wills,' weren't you? I wasn't quite convinced of all that religious mumbo jumbo, not yet anyway, but I'd take inspiration from wherever it came. *Why can't these religious assholes ever just say*

95

what they mean? I grumbled, but I knew what must be done.

It was time to talk to Rubik again. I cast *Commune* and was thrilled to see my six-sided pal float towards me. Vonn had given me an idea for a fantastic question, one I couldn't believe I hadn't asked before.

"Hey Rubik, can you give me a *Boon* that will help me defeat and escape the Agent?"

Apparently, I was getting better at phrasing proper questions as the cubic creature's thoughts invaded my mind with the best *YES* of my life.

It grabbed my head with its rubbery hands, and then the *Boon* of new knowledge filled my brain. I would have collapsed to my knees, but Rubik's noodle arms possessed far more strength than expected.

My mind expanded in a nova of potential and then shrank into a singularity of possibility. It exploded and reformed a thousand upon a thousand times. Just as I knew my very being would burn away it was over.

I collapsed to the ground as drool dribbled from my suddenly parched mouth. I dry heaved and choked and fell onto my face. A new prompt was blinking in my vision.

You have been granted the Boon Accelerated Learning.

Accelerated Learning gives you a 500% increase to learning or training of one skill of your choice.

This Accelerated Learning will last for one full day.
Any Stamina cost associated with the skill chosen is negated for the duration of the Boon.

"Rubik, you are the man, or... whatever," I said as I opened my desert dry eyes and stood. Normally, Rubik would have already floated away, but once again he was ogling me with his unblinking up and down stare. "Oh, right I said, payment."

I dug into my pack and pulled out the *Writ of Cerrunos* again. Rubik looked at the book and back to me, and somehow, I knew it was no longer interested in the book.

Perhaps time moved differently for it as well.

I rustled through my pack, seeking something else to offer it, when I felt it grab my head again. This time he held me in a single hand that was far stronger than logic suggested it should be. It brought its other hand up and the three stumpy digits I thought of as fingers thinned out into points and moved slowly towards my face.

"Um," I said in alarm as the now very thin and very sharp fingers came directly at my eye. I tried to pull back, but the square bastard was incredibly strong. It felt like my head was in a vice. Rubik sunk its talons into the flesh around my eye and I screamed.

The pain went on for many long seconds and then with a pop and a squelch I felt my eye being pulled from its socket. Rubik pulled the eye close and looked at it from many angles as I continued to scream. It didn't seem to notice my distress. Just as I didn't think things could get worse, the creature's giant mouth opened again.

"No, no, no, do not do that," I yelled as it moved my stolen eyeball towards the razor-toothed maw. It tossed it inside and the teeth came down with a sickening slurping pop. *This fucking cube just ate my eyeball,* my mind screamed in terror.

Rubik let me go and I fell to the ground, weeping in pain and horror. An odd ripple flowed over the surface of the cube and its eye shrank to the size of a grapefruit and shifted to the left. Then a small dot appeared in the space on the right side of the cube's face and expanded into another eye. It was my eye, just much larger and now it was staring unblinking back at me.

"Aaaaggghhh!" I screamed, and the cube stared at me for a moment, before turning and floating away. The mists faded and time returned to normal. I was back in the inn.

"Aaaaggghhh!"

"Shut up dwarf," Gaarm grumbled. "Hey what happened to your eye?"

"Aaaaggghhh!"

I jumped up and ran towards the front door. I was seriously freaked out, and my peripheral vision was shot. I bumped into people, tables and chairs.

People I knew and hated all stared at me in shock and

alarm, some complaining, some screaming in shock. Apparently, a man suddenly having no eye was not a normal occurrence, even in this shithole inn.

I finally reached the door and yanked it open to see the Agent standing there. I screamed again, slammed the door in her face and tried to run to the back door. With my vision so jacked up she and her goon were on me in moments.

A bit later I jumped off the bridge again and as I drowned a horrid thought went through my head. *What if I come back still missing the eye?*

Then I died.

9

I set my empty mug down onto the table with a hollow thunk, releasing an unexpected spark of energy that would have made me jump, as it had innumerable times before, but I was a bit preoccupied. My vision seemed normal, but I brought a tentative hand up to my face to make sure. My fingers touched my eye and I let out a whimper of relief.

"Quit crying dwarf," Gaarm said. I looked up to see he and the dealer both waiting for me to decide what to do. Anger surged up inside me and I decided that this time I was going all in. I pushed my coins into the middle of the table. "All in," I said and tossed my card atop the pile.

Gaarm's eyes widened in shock and then suspicion. I could almost see the misfiring neurons in his small brain sending the word cheater to his mouth, but I beat him to the punch.

"Cheater!" I yelled, pointing at the doofus Eldarian. His mouth dropped open to reveal that too often seen gaggle of rotten teeth, but no words came out. Apparently, I'd stumped the bastard.

I opened the prompt that had been blinking since that cubic prick Rubik had torn my eye out.

You have been granted the Boon **Accelerated Learning.**

Which skill do you wish to Accelerate?

I looked directly at Gaarm and said *Analyze*. A torrent of warm energy rushed into my mind, and into my eyes. I saw things in a way I never had before. Every photon of light brought information to my brain. Every breath brought enlightenment.

I turned *Analyze* on and left it on. Normally *Analyze* worked in short bursts. You'd stare all creepy like at someone and activate the skill. Your *Stamina* bar would go down a few ticks and you'd either learn some stuff about your target or you wouldn't.

With no *Stamina* cost, there was no reason to turn it off. The amount of information that poured into my mind was incredible, and for the first time in an unknowable amount of days I wished I wasn't drunk.

I cast my gaze around the room and drank in the information. Now, most of it I already knew from previous trips through the rabbit hole, but this time a tidal wave of prompts came at me and I had to shut them down. At this point I really wasn't trying to glean information from them. I just wanted to grind.

I lived and died dozens of times as I upped *Analyze*. Eventually I grew bored ogling my fellow inn-mates and wandered the town. The first few times I only got about five minutes of staring and ogling in before I came across the Agent, but I soon discovered that if I went the opposite direction from her, I gained another five to ten minutes. That much time was like a vacation in heaven.

I won't bore you with several dozen prompts that poured into my brain over my many lives but suffice to say the folks of Harlan's Watch were as odd a mix of people as you'd encounter anywhere. Some had secret desires that got me feeling' all randy, while others made me blanch and grow queasy.

Several citizens had skills I desired, and I had knowledge I could trade.

You have Learned Skills.

You have reached Level 1 in Air Magic.

You have reached Level 1 in Unarmed.

You have reached Level 1 in Small Blades.

You have reached Level 1 in Divination.

> **You have Learned Skills. (Con't)**
>
> *You have reached Level 1 in Alchemy.*
> *You have reached Level 1 in Disarm Traps.*
> *You have reached Level 2 in Smithing.*

Several townsfolk helped me up my skills, some unwilling.

> **Your Skills have Levelled.**
>
> *You have reached Level 19 in Stealth.*
> *You have reached Level 18 in Dodge.*
> *You have reached Level 13 in Pickpocket.*

I even helped a few people.

> **You have Completed a Quest.**
>
> *You have been awarded 100 XP for the secret quest **Teach a Boy to Pilfer**.*
>
> *You have taught the street urchin Furrick how to Pickpocket. He will now be able to steal enough to feed himself and his young sister Ariaan. You have made him promise to only steal from "douche bags and asshats."*

Pay it forward I say.

The sheer amount of information my brain was taking in gifted me with an ever-present headache, but I pushed through. I'd paid a heavy price for this *Boon* and I was gonna make the most of it. Soon I earned my reward.

> **Your Skills have Levelled.**
>
> *You have reached Level 50 in Analyze.*

Decision time was upon me. I had a whopping 8 *Perk Points* to spend, and a whole slew of new *Skills* to tempt my consumerism. But, I had been working towards one goal since I first checked out the *Analyze Perk Tree*. Without hesitation I put points into the *Know Falsehoods, False Report 2* and *Spell Osmosis*. That left me with 5 Perk Points and many levels to go in Analyze. It was time to grind.

My new *Perks* led me to discover a kinder, gentler, less psycho and bloody way to level. My *Know Falsehoods Perk* really opened some questing opportunities. Most of them were simple enough, delivering love letters, making subtle threats, crafting iron daggers and the like. Quite a few of the folks about town had bounties on their heads, so I became friendly with the local constables.

You have Completed Quests.

*You have been awarded 2,000 XP for completing the quest **Teach a Boy to Pilfer** (x20).*

*You have been awarded 10,000 XP for completing the quest **A Lovely Letter** (x20).*

*You have been awarded 20,000 XP for completing the quest **A Night to Remember** (x20).*

*You have been awarded 1,000 XP for completing the quest **Craft an Iron Dagger** (x20).*

*You have been awarded 200,000 XP for completing the choice quest **Meddle in the Gang War** (x20).*

*You have been awarded 100,000 XP for completing the quest **Bounty for the Pyromaniac** (x20).*

You have Completed Quests. (Con't)

You have been awarded 100,000 XP for completing the quest **Bounty for the Beast Humper** *(x20).*

You have been awarded 100,000 XP for completing the quest **Bounty for the Grave Robber** *(x20).*

You have been awarded 100,000 XP for completing the quest **The Mayor is Corrupt** *(x20).*

And all the while, my *Analyze* skill kept improving. *Accelerated Learning* was an insanely powerful *Boon*, and despite the horrific price I'd paid, I would almost be willing to pay it again. Maybe. *Fuck you Rubik, you creepy-ass cube.*

While I was enjoying my vacation minutes outside the Shining Unicorn Inn, I still had to face off against the Agent and her thralls over and over and over. My *Order Magic* skill kept leveling even though the spells still didn't damage the Agent. It was time to find out why?

The Agent.

Level: 41.
Health: 678.
Stamina: 534.
Mana: 367.
Spirit: 1,000.
Specialty: Agent

The Agent is a servant of the High God Aluran.
Strengths: Small Blades Master. Analyze Master.
Immunities: Complete resistance to all magic cast by opponents of Journeyman or lower level. (Ring).
Weaknesses: Unknown.

The Agent was a complete badass. Not only was she a way higher level than I, she was also a Master in at least two skills.

Even if she was using *False Reports* on me, I knew that her *Strengths* were legit as my own *False Reports 2* made me immune to any falsehoods she could have masked her *Strengths* with.

I would have been less certain about her *Immunities*, knowing that she could *False Report* me, but anecdotal evidence suggested that her *Immunities* were accurate. And even more interesting, they apparently came from a ring she wore. I would do my damned best to get my hands on that ring before this day was done.

Why wouldn't she create a *False Report* on her *Immunities*? Did she believe that nobody could have a high enough *Analyze* skill to peer through her veils of secrecy? Was she that arrogant and cocksure? Perhaps that would be her undoing.

Another possibility went through my mind. Perhaps she had spent all her *Perk Points* on the more aggressive skills. She clearly had bolstered her *Short Blades* skill with a variety of Perks. Maybe she didn't have all the *Analyze Perks* that I did.

I noted, that like Vonn, she had a specialty. She was an Agent. That one was a giant no duh, but I had no idea what it meant. Maybe, before I killed her I'd ask, real nice like.

I still needed to up my *Analyze* skill. If I could become a Master, I might steal some useful skills from her. Just for fun I blasted her with an *Order Bolt*. As expected it did nothing to her, but the effects on the thralls was another thing altogether. I loved killing those mute bastards.

You have earned Experience.
You have earned 152,300 XP for slaying the Agent's Thrall (x100)

Your Skills have Levelled.
You have reached Level 26 in Order Magic.

Yet, I still had a long way to go. I know, I know; I'm getting a bit sick of it too, trust me. But one can't hack the *Game Mechanics*. Let's just say I kept plugging away, grinding, completing quests, meeting the townsfolk of Harlan's Watch and finding new and fun ways to kill the Agent's pals. After a lot of sweat, tears, blood, vomit, headaches, screams, squeals, occasional baby talk and many, many deaths, I earned the most amazing prompt of my life.

Your Skills have Levelled.

You have reached Level 75 in Analyze.

You have reached Level 16 & 17.

You have 10 unused Attribute Points.
You have 7 unused Perk Point. (2 New and 5 Previously Earned)

You have reached Master Tier in Analyze.

You can now see the Strengths, Immunities and Weaknesses of anyone successfully Analyzed.
At Master Tier the Stamina requirement for Analyze is reduced to 5 points.
You have also opened the secret Master Tier Perk Branch Prediction.

I jumped up and down and danced in the streets, reaffirming several townsfolk's belief that I'd make an excellent village idiot. I didn't care, I'd leveled enough to ensure that my original plan was doable, but there was a new wrinkle. Reaching *Master Tier* had opened up a secret *Perk Branch* called *Prediction*, and boy was that branch appealing.

Analyze Perk Tree.

-----Prediction-----
Those who invest in the Prediction branch of the Analyze Perk Tree can gain such incredible insight into an opponent that they can predict their actions. All Prediction Perks require that the user be of an equal or higher Tier than the opponent or creature to be effective.

Analyze Perk Tree. (Con't)
Avoidance enables the user to predict an attack by an enemy and therefore avoid the attack. It feels like a sudden ability to sense danger coupled with a short burst of credible information about what to do to avoid the attack.
Foresight enables the user to not only predict and avoid an attack but also know what action to take next.
NOTE: *All Secret Perk Tree Perks require 2x Perk Points to acquire.*   NOTE: *All Secret Perk Tree Perks require 50 Stamina to activate.*

"Damn," I said, channeling my inner Chris Tucker in *Friday*. The *Prediction Perks* were incredible. As I read about *Avoidance*, I grinned. This had to be the trick the Agent had been using since we first met, oh so many loops ago. I dumped 2 Perk Points into *Avoidance* so quickly I'm surprised I didn't pull something. "I got you now, bitch."

Analyze Perk Tree.			
Tier	Understanding	Defense	Learn
Base	Detect Falsehood	Block Analyze	Skill Resistance 1
Apprentice	Know Desires	False Report 1	Skill Resistance 2
Journeyman	Know Falsehoods	False Report 2	Spell Osmosis
Master	Know Skills	False Report 3	Skill Osmosis
Grandmaster	Know Perks	False Report 4	Perk Osmosis

Analyze Hidden Perk Tree
Prediction (2x Points)
N/A
N/A
N/A
Avoidance
Foresight.

I dumped more points into *Know Skills, False Report 3* and *Skill Osmosis.* I was becoming a complete, if non-traditional, badass. I thought back to my conversation with Vonn about the difficulty of leveling *Analyze* and wondered just how few people in the Realms could do the things I could now do? Maybe this hell loop wasn't so bad after all.

This hyper specialization, this niching down into one skill with all my focus had grown out of necessity, but I now imagined the possibilities it granted me. I could likely defeat opponents of much higher levels with these *Perks.* Through information, and perhaps more importantly disinformation, I could pick and choose my battles, when to fight them and when to end them.

The one downside of *Avoidance* was the staggering *Stamina* cost. I dumped all 10 *Attribute Points* into *Constitution.*

Lex - Level 17	Stats
Ordonian Deity: Cerrunos Experience: 1,552,400 Next Level: 247,600	Health: 192 Stamina: 206 Mana: 234 Spirit: 183
Attributes	**Gifts**
Strength: 23 Constitution: 39 Dexterity: 17 Intelligence: 61 Wisdom: 16 Attribute Points: 0 Perk Points: 2	Player Tracking (Gryph) Ordonian Bloodlust **Immunities**: +25% to Order Magic. **Weaknesses**: -25% to Chaos Magic

I only had 2 Perk Points left. My *Order Magic* skill was my next most powerful, but I knew that I needed to reach *Journeyman* level before my spells would affect the Agent.

I looked at all my skills and decided my best option would be *Blunt Weapons*. I'd have to hope that the *Avoidance Perk* would allow me to be shifty enough to use my war hammer effectively. If I was right, I might finally defeat the Agent.

Blunt Weapons Perk Tree.

-----Crushing Blow-----

When activated, Crushing Blow has a 20% chance per Tier to land a crushing blow. Crushing Blow does not add to damage, but it will deliver a series of debuffs and can be combined with other Blunt Weapon Perks.

At Grandmaster Level it becomes Paralyzing Blow, which provides all the effects of Crushing Blow 4 + a 50% chance to paralyze an enemy for 2 minutes.

Effects: Successfully landing Crushing Blow causes the opponent to receive the following debuffs: -5 to Intelligence, Dexterity and Wisdom per Tier for 30 seconds. -10% chance to hit per Tier for 20 seconds. Victim cannot activate any Perks for 10 seconds per Tier.

Blunt Weapons Perk Tree. (Con't)

-----**Speedy Blow**-----

When activated, Speedy Blow has a 20% chance per Tier to beat an opponent's attack. This not only negates the attack but also catches the opponent off guard, resulting in a 50% penalty to their next attack. Opponents can deduct their Dexterity Attribute from the percentage chance of success.

-----*Damage Bonus*-----
Bonus to damage.

I put a point into *Crushing Blow and another into Damage Bonus*. Speedy Blow sounded great too, but the Agent had a far higher *Dexterity* than me, so it had limited usefulness, for now.

Blunt Weapons Perk Tree			
Tier	Crushing Blow	Speedy Blow	Damage Bonus
Base	Crushing Blow 1	Speedy Blow 1	+20%
Apprentice	Crushing Blow 2	Speedy Blow 2	+30%
Journeyman	Crushing Blow 3	Speedy Blow 3	+40%
Master	Crushing Blow 4	Speedy Blow 4	+50%
Grandmaster	Paralyzing Blow	55%	+60%

I used the last few free minutes before the Agent found me to create my *False Reports*. I couldn't be sure they'd be effective upon her. For all I know she had the same *Perks* as I did. But, every bit helped.

I was now Lex, a Level 8 Ordonian Warrior Priest and my *Blunt Weapons Perk Tree* made my war hammer a potent weapon. I considered drifting further from the truth, but my robes and war hammer would be a dead giveaway as to my true nature. It would be better if she underestimated me.

I gave this Lex an *Immunity* to *Thought Magic*, in case I was wrong about the Agent's skill set and she really was reading my mind. She'd probably see through it quick enough, but maybe, just maybe it would buy me some time.

I spent some time thinking on my *Weakness*. What false weakness could I present that would give the real me a tactical advantage?

As the Agent and her thralls walked up to me, an idea popped into my head, and I grinned. I walked with her to the edge of town, knowing that the next time we played this little game, the results would be different.

10⊕

I was back, and I had a lot to do in a short amount of time. The idea for my plan had always been there lurking in the recesses of my mind, but it had taken a shift of mindset for me to see the path forward.

The Agent was a Big Boss, and I had to treat her as such. That meant allies. I'd spent a lot of time with the folks in the Shining Unicorn Inn and I was pretty sure I knew what buttons to push to get them to play along.

Arno, the fire mage was an easy one. I agreed to burn the world with him and he was game for pretty much anything. Gaarm and his buddies all had bounties on them, so all I had to do was suggest that the Agent had come for them.

Percinius, the chubby priest was also pretty easy. I'd agree to convert to his religion if he continually cast buffs on me. And to help him over the hump I told him the Agent worshipped chthonic demons. That dude had a hard-on of hate for all things demonic.

Grimslee and Seraphine presented a bit of a pickle. I wasn't sure I could get either one on my side. Seraphine was deadly, especially with that hellacious poison, but I wasn't sure how I could recruit her. If I timed it right, I might call in Master Grimslee's favor, but that meant risking getting the *Secure Scroll* from Seraphine.

In the end I went all out since I literally had all the time in the world. If I didn't get it right, the first time I'd do better the next time. I chatted up Arno and the Priest, my lies getting them on Team Lex. I greased up Gaarm's suspicions by casually mentioning there was a bounty hunter in town.

"Apparently she's searching for some dude who had his way with a Duke's cattle." Gaarm said nothing, but his eyes widened in panic. I'm pretty sure he was primed and ready and would go where I pointed him.

I used *Pickpocket* on Seraphine and gave the *Secure Scroll* to Master Grimslee, making him promise to hear me out. His eyes widened and snapped to his barmaid, but he kept his word and listened to my offer. I'd take his favor now, and later, he and I would take down Seraphine together. I could see his anger burning inside him, but nobody became a power player in a mob syndicate by being stupid. He turned his anger inward and agreed to my plan.

I looked to Vonn's empty seat and wished my buddy was still here. That's when a thought hit me. Had I made Vonn up? I had gone a bit looney tunes there for a bit. Endless mass murder can do that to you. A chill moved through my body at the thought.

What if I'd gone all *Shutter Island*? What if all these adventures, this entire tale, was a figment of my crazed imagination?

I looked around the room, and the icy feeling settled into my gut, chilling me to the core. All the actors were playing their roles. Seraphine even smiled at me, tracing her hand along my arm and pausing.

"You okay hon'?" she asked.

I looked into her eyes, knowing that sweet, warm exterior was a facade, a veneer of bullshit. I smiled.

"You ever feel you're just an actor in a very badly written play?" I asked her.

"Every morning when I wake up," she said with a grin. "But, what can you do? You either play the role you're given, or you get kicked out of the show."

She was right. I had no way of knowing if this was real or not, so I just had to stay true to me. *I have to protect Gryph.*

"Oh, shut up, you effing dickhead subconscious," I mumbled and looked up at Seraphine.

"I've got a contract for you." Her eyes widened in surprise, and her hand went to the dagger I knew she had hidden in her apron. "2,000 gold if you kill the small elf woman about to walk through the door."

"I don't know what you're…" she said.

"Daffodil," I said. Seraphine pushed herself up to me. All eyes in the inn would think the flirtatious look on her face was genuine, if misguided, but I felt the tip of her dagger near my heart.

"Why shouldn't I kill you now?"

"I can think of two reasons. One, Grimslee knows about you and plans to kill you after this is through. Help me kill the woman about to walk through that door and I'll help you kill Grimslee. Second, you like money, and I know where he hides his stash. You can have it all."

Her thoughts spun behind those cold, grey eyes. Then I felt the dagger point ease its pressure. Her warm smile returned, and her eyes grew warm and flirty once more.

Damn, she's good.

"You got a deal hun," she said.

I leaned in close. "One more thing, use the Bane of Life on the Agent. That stuff is horrid." Shock filled her eyes as she tried to understand how I knew what I knew. But then she smiled, and I suspected the moment she had her money, she'd kill me too.

It was time, and I set my gaze upon the door and waited. My heart thundered in my chest and I pulled *Mana* into my hands, ready to cast *Order Bolt*. I looked to Arno, the Priest, Seraphine and Master Grimslee. Everything was ready.

The door opened, and the Agent walked in. She scanned the room and soon found me. She smiled a warm smile that almost seemed genuine.

Her thrall stepped in behind her and I fired *Order Bolts* from both hands. She didn't move, knowing full well that my attack could not hurt her. What she couldn't know was that I knew that as well. The shards of white energy zipped towards her and then flashed around her, taking her thrall in the face.

A scowl crossed the Agent's face when she realized that I was not aiming at her. I felt a tickle flow over me and knew that she was using *Analyze* on me. I fed her my *False Report* and watched as a smile grew across her face. *She's taken the bait.*

A warm glow surrounded me.

Buff Added.

---

*Percinius, the Priest of Ferrancia has cast **Wellbeing** on you. +25% to Stamina Regeneration. +25% to Health Regeneration.*

Master Grimslee's crossbow twanged, and the Agent activated *Avoidance* stepping aside, a second before the bolt would have hit her in the neck. This time I could see a faint blur the instant before she moved, and I also knew which direction she would move. I wondered if that was because my *Analyze* skill was so high, or because I possessed the *Avoidance Perk*.

"Gaarm, Bounty hunter!" I yelled.

Gaarm's eyes shot to me and then to where I pointed. He stood and growled, drawing his dagger and rushing the Agent. His fellow thugs followed suit. In moments they surrounded the Agent.

Arno unleashed two torrents of *Flames* from his palms, his face a grim visage of crimson insanity. The jets of fire impacted the roof of the inn, directly above the Agent's head and quickly ate away at the support beams.

It had taken some convincing to get Arno to agree to not attack the Agent directly. I knew she was immune to the magical damage the spell caused, but I suspected that protection did not extend to being crushed by flaming wreckage.

I fired several more volleys of *Order Bolt* at the thrall. He'd collapsed to one knee but was already getting back to his feet. The barrages of energy punched into his face over and over and he stumbled back through the door and landed in the street. A prompt told me he was no longer of this world.

You have earned Experience.

You have earned 1,523 XP for slaying the Agent's Thrall.

The Agent drew her swords and in a green blur of motion, several things happened in quick succession. She cleaved Arno's head from his body, stopping the flames.

Gaarm attacked, but the Agent activated *Avoidance* again and she stepped aside. Her other blade sliced through Gaarm's arm. He fell screaming and his goons quickly followed in a whirlwind of motion that removed arms, severed legs, and punctured throats and split skulls.

I had no idea what kind of swords she wielded, but daddy wanted. I made a mental note to grab those as well. All the while I could see the Agent using *Avoidance*. Her *Stamina* was being drained like a bucket with a hole in it, dear Liza.

So far, so good.

A few minutes later she'd taken care of Gaarm's thugs and she stared at me with that same crazed look I first saw in the alley when this shit day first started.

It seemed so long ago.

The cracking of burning wood drew my attention back and the ceiling above the Agent collapsed. She activated *Avoidance* again and ran forward as the flaming wreckage hit the ground behind her.

I could see the sheen of sweat on her skin and she was breathing in great ragged gasps. She was still standing, but her *Stamina* was bottoming out. This was my chance. I gripped my hammer with both hands and ran towards her. She came at me, no fear in her eyes.

Good, I hope.

I took a moment to activate my *Racial Gift, Ordonian Bloodlust*. I felt a boiling rage churn through me, and I felt vibrant and alive and powerful, and dumber.

She pumped green energy into her boots and leapt over the table. I swung my hammer in a wide arc. There was no way I could miss. But guess what, I did. She activated *Avoidance* again and with the slightest of toe taps on the table's surface she flipped up and over me.

My swing took me off balance and I stumbled forward. She lashed out with one of her swords and I felt the razor-sharp blade slice through the Achilles tendon of my left leg. I fell to the ground, barely keeping my hands on my hammer. I hobbled back to my feet, and the Agent danced out of the range of another clumsy swing. This time she didn't use *Avoidance*. She didn't need to.

I stood and felt the warm glow of the Priest's healing spell knit my tendon and muscle and the pain eased.

Thank you Percinius.

I stood and pressed my attack, swinging my hammer. She used *Avoidance* again and side stepped my blow. She spun and brought her sword low for another attack against my legs, but this time I used *Avoidance*.

The look in her eyes as I sidestepped her attack was like a gift from the gods. I brought the shaft of my hammer up and into her face, earning a wondrous crack from her nose. She stumbled back, the shock stunning her mind clear on her face.

So, you may be wondering what my *False Weakness* was? It was kinda genius if I do say so. Like any good lie, it held an element of truth.

When she'd *Analyzed* me, she learned that I had no access to my *Spirit* energy, since I had 'betrayed my god.' In my mind it was the other way around. That dick had up and died on me.

Regardless she was wrong. I had so much *Spirit* that a high school cheer squad at the state championship would seem tame in comparison, and the Agent was about to get a face full of that *Spirit*.

I dumped as much *Spirit* into my hammer as I could and eyeballed her. This part of the plan was tricky and required perfect timing. I gave Grimslee the predetermined signal, and the crossbow twanged. As I'd hoped the Agent used *Avoidance* stepping forward as the speeding bolt zipped behind her.

I swung my hammer in a ferocious upwards arc and activated *Crushing Blow 1*. The hammer impacted her chin just as the bolt thunked into the wall a few feet behind her.

I felt the bones of her face crumple and she would have screamed if my hammer hadn't shattered her jaw. She flew backwards, landing on the table where Gaarm and I had played so many pleasant games. Cards and coins scattered, and a couple of lovely, lovely prompts popped into my mind.

You have achieved a Critical Hit against the Agent.
5 x Damage

> **You have achieved a Crushing Blow 1 against the Agent.**
>
> *Damage: (41 Base + 24 Spirit) x 5 Critical Hit Bonus = 325 Crushing Blows are dealt by Blunt Weapons and result in concussion like symptoms.*
>
> *-5 to Dexterity, Intelligence and Wisdom for 30 seconds.*
>
> *-25% chance To Hit for 20 seconds.*
>
> *Victim cannot activate Perks of any kind for 10 seconds.*

I couldn't load my hammer with *Spirit* for the next 11 seconds, so I just smashed, smashed the old-fashioned way. I brought my hammer down again and again. Each time the Agent partially blocked my attacks, but the damage was adding up.

The Agent stood and stumbled backwards. I had to give her credit. She was tough as nails. Her face was a bloody wreck and her eyes, once filled with amused certainty, now held a fierce anger.

She jumped at me with incredible speed and sunk both of her sword tips into my shoulders. They weren't fatal blows, and weren't meant to be, but they forced me to drop my hammer. She twisted the swords and agony surged through me as the blades dug deeper into my shoulders.

I laughed through the pain, which trust me is difficult to do, and said a single word. Unfortunately, the sound was a mere croak in my throat. This confused the hell out of her, and she leaned in close attempting to hear what I'd said.

"I said, Seraphine." And I laughed again.

Perhaps it was the unexpected nature of the attack, or the debuffs she suffered that made her dumb, or her *Stamina* was so low that she couldn't activate *Avoidance*, but she didn't sense the wily barmaid assassin appear behind her until the dagger punctured up and into her side.

"Hey sweetie," Seraphine whispered as the blade sunk home. "You should be nicer to my man." Seraphine winked at me.

The Agent's look of shock quickly turned to agony as the acidic poison *Bane of Life* shredded her body. I knew what that poison felt like, so I almost felt sympathy for her. But, that feeling quickly faded. This bitch had put me through the hell of a thousand deaths. It was high time I returned the favor.

I kicked her to the ground and Seraphine pulled one, then the other sword from my shoulders. Then Percinius was there, healing me. I stared down on the Agent as her body spasmed in pain. I could see black lesions form and spread across her skin as the poison ate away at her flesh.

"Why does Aluran want to find Gryph?" I asked. She either didn't hear me or was ignoring me, so I tapped her none too lightly with my hammer. "Hey, what does Aluran want with Gryph?"

Amazingly, she laughed. "Your buddy, your pal, your Gryph is the key to everything," she said coughing up blood and black acidic gore. "And you're going to help us find him." More coughs and spasms wracked her body.

"You're pretty confident for someone about to die."

She laughed again and then she began glowing. It started low, like the dim illumination of a kid reading under the covers with a flashlight, but it quickly flared to a blinding brightness, more potent than a noonday sun.

I squinted against the light and heard her speak.

"My High God Aluran grant me your Boon." The light exploded, and a wall of force pummeled into me. I stumbled and fell.

Falling onto my ass was becoming a too frequent habit.

I blinked, trying to clear my eyes. I couldn't make out anything except one blob swung at another blob. Something rolled towards me and bounced between my legs.

I scrunched my eyes shut and after another moment they cleared enough for me to see the Agent standing, fully healed, both swords held point down. At her feet lay Seraphine's decapitated corpse. I looked down to see Seraphine's head resting in my crotch. I screamed and crawled backward.

"Nice try kiddo, but there is no stopping me. I do as the High God wills."

Then she walked towards me. My brain must have demanded answers that my conscious mind was too stunned to ask because suddenly I had used *Analyze*.

The Agent has used the Gift Boon of the High God Aluran.

Cost: *1,000 Spirit.*

All Debuffs instantly neutralized. All wounds instantly healed.

All Stats refilled. +25% to Health, Stamina, Mana and Spirit regeneration for one day.

This is a single use Boon.

"Crap," I said as she came at me. I stood and tried to run, but she was on me in seconds. She punched me in the face with the pommel of her sword and I blacked out.

I came to a bit later, arms tied behind my back. I was swaying back and forth, and my stomach felt queasy. *Am I on a boat?* I thought and quickly felt dumb as Lurch tossed me over his shoulder. We were getting close to the bridge.

"Hey," I croaked through a parched throat.

"Stop, get him on his feet," I heard the Agent say, and Lurch tossed me off his shoulder and onto the dusty ground. I grunted in pain. "I said get him on his feet, not throw him on the ground. Do not damage the merchandise."

I felt rough hands pull me to my feet and then spin me towards the Agent. She walked up to me, all smiles and grins.

"That was a lot more exciting than I expected, well done."

"Um, thanks," I said, depression pumping into me. I had given it my all, and I was still in the same damn place I'd been so many other times. I was sick of dying. I was sick of living an endless loop. I was sick of all of it.

11

I set my empty mug down onto the table with a hollow thunk, releasing a completely expected spark of energy. This time I didn't jump. Gaarm still grinned though and then he sucked at some bit of food in his rancid teeth, all the while staring directly at me. He pushed his pile of coins forward.

"I'm all in," he said.

I sat in silence, staring down at the card in front of me, and I heard both the dealer and Gaarm complain about my inaction, but I didn't care.

"I'm never gonna win," I said and tossed the card face up on the pile.

Oohs and ahs filled the room and I heard Gaarm's chair scrape as he launched himself to his feet.

"I fold," I said and walked towards the front door, my head hung low. I bumped into Seraphine, sloshing her tray of mugs. She looked at me, first with anger, then with a look that almost seemed genuine concern.

"You okay hun?"

I mumbled something like an apology and tugged at my beard. Then I opened the door and walked into the cool evening.

For the first time I really looked at the town of Harlan's Watch. It was pleasant and quaint, and the residents seemed like decent enough folks. Ya know except for the murderers, rapists, mob bosses, pyromaniacs, assassins, religious zealots and livestock molesters. They were just people going about their lives with no idea of the violence that had occurred over and over in their midst.

I wanted nothing to do with any of it. I'd lived this day so many times I'd lost count. I'd died so many times and killed so many people in so many ways that I could not be sure I hadn't lost my mind.

Maybe I'd wake up under the table in Master Grimslee's

inn and learn it had all been a mead-fueled dream. I doubted it, but it was possible. Ultimately it didn't matter, cuz I was tired, and I couldn't do it anymore. It was time to surrender.

I found the Agent and told her I'd go without a fuss.

"I'll go peacefully this time," I said. She gave me an odd look. "Oh yeah, for you this is the first time."

She cocked her head in suspicion and then nodded at Lurch. They tied my hands and led me over the bridge.

"I can't do this anymore. I'm sorry Gryph," I said, looking skyward as if expecting a benevolent face of my missing Player to form in the clouds and look down upon me with forgiveness.

"So, his name is Gryph? We didn't know that."

Shit, my stupid big mouth. I felt like the biggest douche at the douchebag convention.

The Agent removed the port stone from a hidden pocket and tossed it up in the air, catching it like it was a mere trinket.

"See that hill up ahead?" she asked.

"Yeah," I mumbled. "It's where the townsfolk execute folks."

"Yes," she said with a grin. "I like people who know their history."

We started up the incline leading to the hill, and I stopped, realizing that where I now stood was the farthest I'd been since arriving in the Realms. I was leaving my old life behind, like a juvenile delinquent shipped off to military school. With a sigh I stepped forward and into, what I was sure, would be a short, intense life.

We walked up the hill where the remnants of an old gallows poked skyward like the rotten teeth of some long-buried beast. This place had the stink of death, but I barely noticed.

The Agent turned and motioned for Lurch to bring me closer. He pushed me well past the boundary's decorum set for personal space and I found myself nose to nose with the short elf woman. She was at least an inch taller than I was.

"This isn't really doing much for my self-esteem," I said, indicating the height similarity.

"Cheer up pal, you have no idea how important you are."

She smiled and then leaned forward. I cringed, imagining her taking a bite out of my face, but instead she pecked me lightly on the cheek. "Thank you for making this so easy."

"Um, sure thing." I said, shoulders slumping even more. She took a firm grip of my shoulder.

"Close your eyes, porting can sometimes make one a bit queasy."

She looked down on the stone as multicolored lights swirled across its surface. Perhaps it was some last remnant of rebellion inside me, but I refused to shut my eyes.

The world folded in and around itself as light expanded and contracted at the same time. Up became down, left became right and then we shifted.

I fell to my knees and everything that had been in my stomach decided it wanted to play the shifting game as well. I bent over and retched for nearly a minute, a thin stream of bile drooling from my mouth.

"Told you," she said. "It's been grand Lex. Maybe I'll see you around."

"Wait, what?"

I watched the Agent exit through a door at the back of the room. After a few moments the world stopped spinning, and I stood. I was on a large open-air balcony overlooking a crystal blue ocean.

The smell of the sea mingled with the noise of seabirds. I realized I was high above a wondrous city, near the top of a tall tower. The beauty of the place was at odds with how I felt, terrified, angst ridden and guilty.

I was so enamored of the sight before me that I nearly didn't hear the small pop nor feel the rush of air. A moment later a tall and magnificent man walked up beside me. I would have jumped, had I possessed the energy to do so.

"Hello Lex," the man said, giving me the winning smile that had won him millions of worshippers. This was Aluran the High God of the Pantheon, and even in the simple robes he wore, he was magnificent.

He had to be six foot five, and possessed a wiry frame laden with muscle, built for both power and speed. After spending half a century in the Realms, I was sure the man could smite me a dozen ways over without breaking a sweat.

Every movement was one of ease, one of power.

Yet, his eyes are what caught my attention. Light blue, almost grey, and possessed a deep intelligence and an odd calm. He looked less despotic conqueror and kinder and wiser religious leader. Somehow that was more terrifying. What's more, he looked exactly as he had on Earth. He was not hiding in the shadows behind a false face.

I used *Analyze*.

Analyze has failed.

Expected as much.

"Sup Bechard?" I said, wondering where my haughty arrogance had come from. After all, I was taunting a god.

He cocked his head, examining me like a cat that found a rat in the basement. "Interesting," he said. "You remember your previous self."

Shit, my damn mouth.

"You're not supposed to, you know that? Banner NPC's are programmed as trusted companions for their Players, who fully believe they are natives of the Realms."

He stared at me some more and I felt the tingle of *Analyze*. I hoped my previously set *False Reports* were still active, and that Aluran wasn't a Grandmaster at the skill. A small scowl crossed his face, but his pleasant smile quickly returned.

"The enigmas grow."

"I'm special," I said, again forcing a cocksure attitude I did not feel into my words.

"Yes, apparently you are. But we'll get to that soon." He turned from the wondrous vista. "Would you care for some refreshment? From what I understand, you've had a bit of a rough day."

I turned to see a table covered in foodstuffs of all kinds, and for the first time in my life my stomach grumbled. I hadn't eaten since my lunchtime sausage roll unless you counted that prize nugget I'd found in my beard. That meant I hadn't eaten in what must have amounted to years.

"I'm starving," I said and sat.

Aluran waved a hand and his seat moved back. He sat, and it moved up to the table. A steward approached and poured a small amount of red wine into the High God's glass. Aluran lifted the glass, swirled the goblet and brought it to his nose. He inhaled, and a satisfied smile turned the corner of his mouth up. Then he took a sip and nodded to the steward who finished the pour. He then came to my side of the table and poured a glass for me.

"You know, this is what I will miss the most about Earth. I've had my vintners working on this for nearly five decades." He took another sip. "It is close, but not quite the same. The wines of Earth cannot be replicated here in the Realms. Something to do with the soil."

"Terroir," I said and took a sip of my own glass.

Now, I know, you're wondering, how did I know it wasn't poisoned? Well, I didn't, but I was pretty sure His Eminence the High Douche didn't bring me all this way just to kill me.

What about truth serum buddy?

Crap didn't think of that. But, by this point I no longer cared.

Aluran raised an eyebrow and nodded to me. "You are different."

"Is that why you brought me here?"

"Perhaps I just wanted the company of someone from the old country." Aluran said with a grin and took another swig of the wine. He sighed in genuine appreciation. "It is so difficult to find quality dinner guests these days. Everybody is too afraid to offend me."

"Life is tough when you're a god."

"Yes, yes, it is," Aluran said with a grin. "But forgive me, you aren't here to listen to me pontificate."

The steward pulled the lid off the High God's plate and Aluran grabbed his knife and fork and indicated I should do the same.

"Please."

The steward came to my side of the table and lifted mine as well. Beneath was a steak that would make Bobby Flay drool. I picked up my utensils and ate.

The food was amazing, and I said so in the few moments I had between bites. "But, I suspect you did not bring me here just for dinner."

"No, I am here to help you, or to be accurate I'm here to

help Gryph."

"If you were trying to help, why did you send the Maiden of Death after me?"

"Anveryn can be a bit overzealous, but she is a deeply loyal ally." Aluran held a bit of rare beef up in front of his face, staring at it as the blood dripped down the tines of his fork. "That is something I believe you know a bit about."

I must protect Gryph. I really hated that voice in my head. "It's true, Gryph and I are buds."

"But, it is more than that, isn't it?"

I felt his eyes bore into mine as if he were seeing into my soul. Did I even have a soul? Apparently whatever answers he sought, were buried too deep, or simply didn't exist, because he returned his attention to his meal. Perhaps I was just a machine after all.

"I struggled with my decision you know," Aluran said, taking another sip from his wine. "I believe that all beings should have free will, but when I returned, the Realms were in chaos. The people suffered under the oppression of corrupt gods. I needed an army that was loyal, not to me, but to an ideal. Sadly to ensure that freedom for others, I had to impose limits to the freedom of your kind. I am sorry for that."

I said nothing and cut another piece of my steak. I looked at it and knew that if Gryph and I were on the brink of starvation that I would give him this piece.

Was it real loyalty, real emotion, or simply lines of code that forced me to feel and to behave in predetermined ways? I thought back to my time with Brynn and Sean, and the instance that I must be programmed for loyalty. They had stolen my free will. How were they any different from the god who sat across from me?

I forced these thoughts down. They were not helping. I could cry to my therapist later if there was a later. "So, if you say you want to help Gryph, why did you attack us when we entered the Realms?"

A look of genuine regret crossed Aluran's face.

"It was fear. Even now, I still struggle with my impulses and I've had this power much longer than Gryph. When I learned what he possessed, ancient fears rose in me. I was desperate to stop him going down the inevitable path of destruction. He does not understand the power he possesses. And if he isn't shown how to control it, it will destroy him."

"And you want to, what, train him?"

"Yes. I know that is hard to believe." Aluran sighed, leaned forward onto both elbows and looked directly at me. "The power Gryph possesses once seduced me, and I knew what it was. He cannot possibly understand what a Godhead is capable of. If he is not taught how to tame the power it will seduce him, it will destroy him. It will eat him from the inside and rend his soul. Power is a drug more potent than any opiate."

I thought back to recent events and knew Aluran was right. I had only a small taste of power in my endless time loop, and what had I done with it? I'd killed repeatedly, with no remorse and no consequences. It had become addictive.

"Gryph is a good man," I said, annoyed at how lame my voice sounded.

"So was I."

I was wondering if I'd gotten this whole thing wrong. What if Aluran spoke the truth? What if the Source had put me right here so that I could help Gryph?

I must protect Gryph.

Shut it, internal programming.

"Why should I trust you?"

"It is the eternal problem of mortal life. You must reach out with trust before you know if you can trust."

"That's not helping me dude." If Aluran was offended by my lack of respect, he didn't show it.

"I will lower my *Analyze* defenses and let you decide for yourself."

He closed his eyes and looked inward. A moment later he opened them again and indicated I should *Analyze* him. I did, and I also used *Know Desires, Know Falsehoods* and *Know Skills* on him as well.

You have used Know Desires on The High God Aluran.

The High God Aluran wishes to atone for previous mistakes. He wants to protect the people of the Realms from all dangers. Specifically, he wants to help Gryph learn to control his Godhead.

You have used Know Falsehoods on The High God Aluran.

The High God Aluran is not a perfect man, nor a perfect god, but he has no deception in his soul.

I'm not an idiot, well not a complete one anyway, so I knew that I couldn't really trust what I was seeing. He was a god after all, so who knew what abilities he had, and what he could hide. Yet, something was making me believe. Everything Aluran had said about the seductiveness of power was correct. My endless hours of entertainment viewing had taught me nothing if not that.

Aluran's Magical Skills.
Fire: 59
Air: 76
Water: 36
Earth: 55
Chthonic: 23
Empyrean: 76
Chaos: 35
Order: 45
Life: 67
Death: 27
Thought: 78
Aether: 25
Soul: 81

"Holy Shit," I said, and then grumbled to myself that I'd said it aloud. It had taken me an unknowable eternity to get one skill to *Master Tier*. Aluran had leveled every *Magic Skill* to at least *Apprentice Tier*. I guess being a god for 50 years makes anything possible.

Aluran's Martial Skills.
Archery: 76
Small Blades: 56
Long Blades: 83
Staves/Spears: 35

Aluran's Martial Skills. (Con't)

Unarmed: 56

Blunt Weapons: 35

Thrown Weapons: 37

Light Armor: 35

Heavy Armor: 82

Dodge: 73

Block: 65

Stealth: 54

Aluran wasn't just a badass wizard; the dude was also fricking Superman, if the son of Krypton was raised as a Knight of Camelot. His *Long Blades* skill was 83 and his *Heavy Armor* was 82. This dude would be impossible to kill. *Maybe you should accept his help Gryph. It would be better than facing him.*

Aluran's Knowledge Skills.

Alchemy: 55 (J)

Analyze: 77 (M)

Artifice: 67 (J)

Smithing: 77 (M)

Disarm Traps: 23 (A)

Harvest: 45 (A)

Imbuing: 87 (M)

Spell Craft: 53 (J)

Invocation: 75

Perception: 65

Aluran's Knowledge Skills. (Con't)
Divination: 35 (A)
Lock Picking: 35 (A)
Pickpocket: 12 (B)

Okay, this is just getting stupid. I had no way to know if what Aluran was showing me was the truth, but even if he was *False Reporting* me that only meant he was even more powerful. This suggested that Aluran was an open book and the tale that book was telling was 'surrender while you have the chance.'

He hadn't let me *Analyze* him to gain my trust, but to fill my breeches in fear. To make me see that, even if he was bullshitting and intended ill will towards Gryph, it wouldn't much matter. The dude was idiotically overpowered, *but at least my Pickpocket skill was higher than his.*

A Quest Prompt popped into my vision.

You have been offered the Quest: Responsible Use of Power 1.
The High God Aluran has offered you a quest. Tell him where he can find Gryph so that he can help Gryph understand and control the power that he possesses. Accepting this quest will earn you Renown with the High God Aluran. Refusal will earn you Enmity with the High God Aluran AND may put the entire Realms in jeopardy. *Difficulty: Complicated.* *Reward: Renown and Unknown.* *Experience: Unknown.*

I was at a loss for words, and as you have probably guessed, that is a rare thing for me. I had no idea what to do. My loyalty to Gryph was strong, but it was a false loyalty.

I had no free will in the situation. Course when I'd had unfettered free will I used it to kill, kill and kill some more, so maybe I didn't deserve it. But, I found that I believed Aluran. I believe that he feared what Gryph could become if he didn't have a mentor. Part of me even believed that he truly had the best interest of the Realms at heart.

"I can tell that you are not convinced," Aluran said.

"I'm not as dumb as I look," I said, and then grumbled to myself at my self-inflicted insult.

"No, you are not. In fact, you are extraordinary."

My eyes snapped up. "What do you mean?"

"You are brash and immature and sarcastic, but beyond that there is something ancient in you. Something I do not understand."

"Like I said, I'm special."

"Then let me help you too. Gryph, you and I, together we could make the Realms a place of peace and wonder. We can usher in a new golden age."

"How can I trust you?"

Aluran shrugged and looked directly at me. "Ultimately you need to make that decision on your own."

"You're a big help here pal."

Aluran smiled and leaned forward. "If you are willing, I'd like to gift you something. Just a small appreciation for even considering my offer. No strings attached."

"Um sure," I said. "Who doesn't like swag?"

Aluran held his hands together, palms upwards and chanted in a low voice. I could not understand the words he spoke, if they were words at all, but a sphere of golden light grew in his hand.

I saw intricate geometric patterns swirl through streams of words in a language I somehow knew hadn't been spoken in the Realms in millennia. The matrix of light throbbed and pulsed and folded in upon itself. Then it calmed, becoming a mirrored globe of golden energy.

With a gentle shove the ball floated towards me. I scrambled backwards in my chair, but I could not move fast enough. The globe flew at me and impacted my chest. I expected great pain and to be flung from my chair, but instead I felt a warmth of wellbeing that soothed away the pains and the hurts I wasn't aware I'd had until they faded. As comfort eased through my body, a prompt popped into my vision.

This *Boon* was amazing. The High God had given me a way to be immune to his power. I looked at Aluran in shock.

"Quite the olive branch," I said.

"I told you Lex, I just want to make the Realms a better place for all. Yet, I know that we have a power imbalance between us. Hopefully this *Boon* will make you feel more at ease. If you ever feel threatened by me, you can use it to protect yourself."

"Yet, it will only last an hour."

The High God spread his arms wide. "If it were permanent, then the imbalance would still exist"

"Yet tipped in my favor," I said with a nod.

"I want to trust you Lex, but you also need to earn that trust."

"Fair enough."

"Help me help Gryph. Help me help you. There is so much more I can teach you both."

I won't lie and say that I wasn't tempted. That is how power works after all, and make no bones, that is exactly what Aluran was offering me. Again, my mind drifted on a tide of guilt back to my actions in the inn. I'd already proven over and over that I didn't do well with power. Maybe Aluran could help me tame my worst instincts.

But something was still not right. I needed a second opinion. I knew what I had to do, I just didn't know if Aluran would let me do it.

Only one way to find out.

I took a last sip of my wine and held my glass up to the steward. This drew Aluran's attention and the fingers of my left hand, hidden under the table, began to cast *Commune*.

132

Aluran's eyes snapped up to mine, and I felt him use the *Analyze Perk Spell Osmosis* on me. A fierce and invisible battle of wills began and as the mists rolled in and time stopped, I felt sweat trickle from my temple and down my face.

My old pal Rubik floated up, still sporting my stolen eyeball. That one was a bit of a mind screw. How did I still have mine when he also had mine?

Or did he? Was Rubik's physical form living information? If so, it would explain how he possessed my eye, while it still sat snug and cozy in my own skull. Maybe he was like a photocopier of things. After all, I kept all my knowledge and experience each loop, but none of the loot.

Regardless, it was still creepy as all get out being stared at by a giant version of your own eye, but I had no time to ponder that particular quirk of multi realm quantum game mechanics. I was about to ask the most important question of my life.

"Is Aluran the right person to be Gryph's mentor and guide in the Realms?"

NO, Rubik thought directly into my mind.

I felt my body seize up in apprehension and fear. "Shit, what do I do now?" I was so lost in my own worrisome thoughts that I almost failed to notice that Rubik was still here, staring at me with unblinking eyes. I looked at him and he lifted his right arm.

He folded two of his three rubbery fingers down and slowly moved the single digit towards me. I freaked out inside, remembering the last time the cube's fingers had come towards me.

"Um, Rubik old pal, what's up?"

I wanted to back up, but the odd physics of the *Order Realm* made every step back a float forward for Rubik. His finger came to my chest, but this time he did not dig into my flesh and remove bits of me for a mid-day snack.

This time he simply laid his finger above my heart. I looked down and then back up at Rubik's eyes. He held the finger there for a moment and then tapped my chest three times. Then he turned and floated away. The mists faded and time began again.

I nearly jumped from my seat. I felt the tingle of Aluran's

Spell Osmosis Perk and felt a wall of will slam down in my mind. A scowl crossed the High God's face.

"I thought we were getting to be friends?"

"We are," I said, forcing calm into my mind and body. "But, trust is a two-way street."

A small scowl turned Aluran's mouth down, but he quickly banished it and smiled. "You are of course correct."

That's when I saw it, a small mote of darkness in his eyes. I don't think Aluran was lying, even now, but he was not the master of his darker impulses that he played at being.

Perhaps he wanted to help Gryph. Perhaps he wished to make the Realms a better place. But in that moment, I saw the darkness that still lived inside him. I saw it because it was the same darkness that lived in me.

"Gryph needs someone to guide him," Aluran said, his voice all certainty and sincerity.

I brought my hand to my face and stroked at my beard, for all the world acting like a man making a tough decision. But my fingers were busy, searching amidst the tangled strands of matted hair.

They found the small object I'd hidden there and held it in a death grip. I'd pickpocketed the vial of poison off of Seraphine as I'd stumbled from the Shining Unicorn Inn. I knew it was a desperate move and my fingers shook in fear as I pulled my hand away from my beard. I looked up at Aluran trying to stop my hand from shaking.

"That someone needs to be me, Lex. You know it to be true."

"No man, that's my job."

I opened the small vial and drank the horrid black liquid down in a quick gulp.

Debuff Added.

You have been poisoned by the Bane of Life, an acidic poison that is melting your body.

Bane of Life is immune to Counter Agents and renders Healing Spells and Potions ineffective for 10 seconds.

50 Damage per second for 10 seconds.

Knowing what was about to happen made this time far worse. It started with my lips and then bubbled into my mouth and down my throat. My teeth melted, and a hole appeared in my throat. I coughed up blood as the poison boiled away my flesh.

Aluran leaped over the table in a single bound and landed gently next to me. He cast healing spells and quickly scowled as he realized they were ineffective.

"What have you done?" he said in anger, and for the first time, I saw the true Aluran, the dark being he struggled so hard to tame and hide.

He pulled his arm back and punched down with all his might. It was a move of uncontrolled anger and frustration. The stone of the floor next to my head splintered under the angry blow.

Despite the agony tearing through my body I laughed, well I tried to laugh, but that's really damn hard to do when your mouth and throat have melted. What came out was a pathetic pained sputter. So, I did the only other thing I could think of.

I extended both middle fingers and gave the douche the double bird.

12

I was back again where it all started. Mug smacked the table with a shock of energy. Gaarm gave me his stupid grin. "I'm all in," he said, but my mind was elsewhere. I was still in this damned loop. Was this permanent? Was I forever doomed to repeat the same damn day over and over, for all eternity.

"Maybe I should have taken Bechard's offer," I said, doubt creeping through me.

"Hey Dwarf, what do you wanna do?" Gaarm grumbled.

"I'm Ordonian," I said. "Yeah, I know, I know, but trust me that's what it says." I tossed my card on top of the pile of coins and folded.

"But sir, you have the winning hand," the dealer said.

"I cheated and I'm really sorry. It's your lucky day Gaarm."

I stood, walked to the bar and ordered a goblet of Master Grimslee's Eldarian fire wine. I sipped at it while I thought on my predicament. If this time loop I was stuck in was anything like the movie *Groundhog's Day*, then I needed to learn a lesson, or become a better person, or achieve some task before I could break free.

Apparently that task was not telling a god to go fuck themselves as fun as that had been. *I must protect Gryph.* I really did not like that little voice, but after scowling at it and telling it to shut up, something occurred to me like a punch to the gut. The answer had been there the whole time; I'd just lost sight of it through all the murder and mayhem.

"I have to protect Gryph," I said.

"That's what life is all about. Protecting the ones you love," Grimslee said and poured himself a glass. He held his glass up and we toasted. "To Gryph."

"I don't really like the guy," I said and took a sip.

"That's how it works sometimes. I hate my wife most days, but I love her, and I'd kill to protect her."

"You know pal, you may be onto something," I said. Maybe it was that simple. Protecting Gryph wasn't just preventing the Agent from taking me to Aluran. It wasn't just discovering how little I could trust the High God. To truly protect Gryph, and the Realms, I had to change. I had to become a better me. I had to realize that despite being programmed for loyalty, I still had a choice. That choice was to become the mentor Gryph needed.

There was just one more thing I needed to do before I could begin my journey towards enlightenment. I needed to kill the Agent. I can't say why, but I was fairly certain that my internal change had broken the loop. Call it intuition, or perhaps faith. *Dammit Vonn, did you make me a believer?*

I was certain of one thing though; I still needed to kill the Agent. Either I was still in the loop and killing her was the final key, or the loop had already been broken. Which meant if she captured me, I'd likely sing like a baby to Aluran. And if I killed myself in any of the dozen fun ways I'd done in the past, it would be permanent. It felt strange, after dying thousands of times, I suddenly found my life to be very precious. But, it would all be for nothing if the Agent captured me.

I made a few preparations, but now that I had the *Boon* from Aluran I planned to handle the heavy lifting on my own. Part of me wondered just how I'd gained exactly what I needed to defeat Aluran's Agent from the High God himself. I was sure that he knew nothing about the time loop, but it still seems incredibly coincidental.

That's when my eyes fell to Vonn's seat, and I heard his words. "If the Source wills."

"Could it be?" I asked and looked up as if seeking an imaginary higher power. I stood there for a few minutes, trying to find some sign that my insane thoughts might be true. Customers bumped into me, muttering and complaining. I got odd looks and a few curses, but I heard no voice from on high, received no words of wisdom. I got nothing.

"Well, I guess it is up to me then."

I spent the last few minutes before the Agent's arrival saying my goodbyes to my fellow inn-mates. Oddly I would miss them all, even Gaarm. When the Agent entered, I was sitting at Vonn's and my table, legs crossed and hands in my lap. I activated my *Boon Aegis of the High God* and went on the attack. This tale has already had too much blood, so I won't bore you with all the gory details. Suffice to say that with the *Boon*, the Agent had no chance against me. My only weakness was my own *Stamina*, and I had Percinius, the zealot priest for that.

Our battle was titanic, and the Agent remained tough, but soon she understood that I would beat her. I was bathed in a constant glow of Percinius' *Stamina Boost* while her *Stamina* and *Health* were being drained quicker than cosmos at a bachelorette party. Eventually she went down.

This time I blocked my eyes ready for the explosion of light that accompanied her *Boon*. She rose, fully healed and eyed me warily.

"Hey Anveryn, how are things?"

Her eyes widened in shock and then expanded in fear. "How? How did you receive the High God's blessing?"

"We're buds, Aluran and I."

I went on the attack. Trust me, I felt bad about it, especially since she seemed genuinely crushed by the revelation. It is hard being abandoned by those you love, and I felt awful for her.

I knew Aluran hadn't forsaken her, but she would spend the last few moments of her life doubting everything she had ever believed in. Yet instead of making her stop, fall in a heap and cry, she redoubled her attack.

But we both knew it wouldn't be enough, and despite my misgivings I kept up my furious assault. Several times she tried to kill Percinius, and while technically I didn't need him to beat her, I would have felt terrible about getting the dude killed; you know, for real killed. So I did my best to shield him from her, and I mostly succeeded. Eventually the Agent went down again, broken and bleeding and staring at me with disbelief. I almost felt bad for her as I raised my hammer over my head.

"Sorry kid," I said and brought my hammer down on her for the final blow. She died, right there on the hard-packed earth floor of that cruddy inn. This time, it was for real. This time, the loop wouldn't begin again. I felt guilty about that.

I dropped my hammer, and then the shouting started. When I saw you and your buddies I raised my hands above my head.

$$* * * * *$$

"So, you see, my story explains it all," I said. I tried to lean back, but the chains holding my manacled wrists were too short. I tried to look cool, but I was thirsty, my beard really itched, my ass was sore from being parked in this damned chair for hours and the cruddy wool sack they'd given me after confiscating all my stuff was giving me a rash.

"Let me get this straight," the gravel crushing against gravel sound of Chief Constable Nahrman's voice said as he stared with unblinking eyes at me. "You are confessing to, what, 1,000 imaginary murders to explain one actual murder?"

"Wow, is it really that many? You may be better at math than me, so I'll take your word for it. But yeah, I'm confessing."

"And you understand that in Harlan's Watch, murder is a hanging offense?"

"Yup, on the nice hill at the edge of town."

He gave me an intense stare as if he could just look inside and get the answers he needed. He harrumphed in irritation and tried a different tactic. "So, when I found you, you were digging around her corpse. Searching for something?"

"Yup, the *Warrant* she carried."

"The scroll you burned."

I nodded.

"But why burn it and then confess?"

"The *Warrant* was all spelled up with powerful magics. It was her badge of authority. If you had read it, it would have compelled you to bring me to Aluran. You wouldn't have had any choice. So, I used *Flames* and huzzah we're both better off."

"How do you figure that?"

I leaned forward once more. "You're a busy man, right?

Got a town to protect. Could you protect it if you had to spend weeks escorting me to Avernia?"

"No, I could not."

"See, I'm on your side. Plus, didn't all those tips I gave you pan out?"

"You mean the bounties on the murderers, rapists, mob bosses, pyromaniacs, assassins and religious zealots?" The Chief Constable read from the notes his assistant had been taking.

"Don't forget Gaarm the livestock molester.

"I was trying to," he said, face twisted in a scowl.

"Well did they? Pan out?"

"You know they did," Nahrman said with a grunt. "You saw my men bring the whole damn lot of them in. Needed to triple up the cells too. Harlan's Watch just ain't equipped to hold so many criminals at once."

"It is such a nice town."

"So, I'm gonna lay out my problem for ya," the Chief Constable said. "If you're telling the truth, you are the worst mass murderer in the history of the Realms, and you are wanted by the High God Aluran. If you're lying, then you're a criminally insane lunatic."

"An accurate and fair assessment, I'd say."

"That's my moral conundrum, you see. If you are a loon, I can't in good faith execute you. I don't like executing crazy folk. I'd rather send you to the Brothers of Zeckoth, see if they can't jumble your brains back into proper position."

"That sounds awful."

"More awful than being hung?"

"Well maybe equally awful," I said, scratching at my beard again.

"You do ponder that statements like that are gonna lean me towards deciding your brains are all scrambled, right?"

I shrugged.

"On the other side if you are sane, then it is my duty as Chief Constable and a loyal servant of the Pantheon to ship you off to Avernia, due to you making me aware of the *Warrant* issued upon you."

I shrugged again, trying to bury the panic that idea brought to my guts.

"Now, here's another wrinkle, and it's one I don't get. I think you want me to execute you."

"What makes you think that?" I said, knowing my feigned ignorance was not deceiving the Chief Constable.

"My job is to read people, and I am very good at my job."

"And you're mighty handsome as well," I said, giving the man an up and down. He was handsome in the same way a flatulent bulldog was handsome, meaning not at all. He grinned at me the way a man only can when he knows the truth about himself and has accepted that truth.

"You cannot escape, but you'd rather die than give up this Gryph you're protecting. That is something I can respect. And perhaps I can help you."

"Huh?" I said.

The Chief Constable turned to his clerk. "Leave us." The wizened old man looked up in shock, but the Chief Constable was firm. "Now!" The small man collected his papers, quills and ink pots and left the room. "And close the door behind you," the Chief Constable barked. The old man grumbled but did as commanded.

After we were alone, Nahrman sighed and looked at me. "Now, I know you murdered that woman, and perhaps you believed you had just cause to do so. You are driven by a need to protect those you care about. I understand that. What I don't understand is how you still believe you can get away with it? You are not a man who is ready to die, which tells me you don't believe that you will. Care to enlighten me?"

I was becoming uncomfortable. I'd tried *Analyze* on the Chief Constable the moment I'd been brought to him and I'd received quite the interesting prompt. I tried again now and got the same reply.

Analyze has Failed.

*Analyze has been Blocked by the Chief Constable's Gift **Mark of the Law**.*

"You already know that won't work," he said and pulled his sleeve up to show me a tattoo on his forearm. It was a five-pointed star encased in a circle. As I stared at it, the *Mark* glowed.

"As long as I am Chief Constable, this *Mark* will protect me from any use of *Analyze*. Can't have every criminal I bring in knowing what I know. You'd have to have reached *Grandmaster Tier* for Analyze to be effective, and that is something you haven't managed, yet."

"Listen," I said, in a voice that was growing desperate. "I confessed. If you need me to sign something, I'll sign it, but you need to bring me to that hill and hang me before that bitch can get back here."

"So, she was a Player," the Chief Constable said. "I suspected as much."

It had been news to me too. After she lay dead at my feet, I searched through her stuff. The *ring*, the thing that allowed her to ignore my *Order Bolts*, wouldn't come off. Neither did her swords or her armor. The shit was soul bound to her, which could only mean one thing. She was a Player, and after she respawned, she'd be back. I rustled a few non-soul bound things off her body before I was arrested, but most of it was useless, and was confiscated.

"I didn't know she was a Player, not until after I'd killed her. How'd you know?"

"A few hours after we arrested you her body dissolved."

"Dissolved?" My face screwed up in disgust.

"Into a rancid puddle of goo. It made quite the mess, and the smell was damn awful, even drove our undertaker from the room." The Chief Constable leaned forward and looked me right in the eye. "Are you a Player? Is that why you want me to execute you?"

I considered lying, telling the man what he wanted to hear, but somehow, I knew he'd see right through me. "No, I'm not a Player, I'm an NPC."

"Hmmm," he said. "You do know that NPCs don't come back from beyond the Grey Veils, right?"

"I do," I said, and a huge grin crossed my face.

"Yet, you still want me to execute you?"

142

"Yes," I said. "I'm tired and I've failed. My only chance of protecting Gryph now is to get away from that bitch, permanently."

"Okay, well I can't grant you that wish. To be honest, I don't think I could stop it if I wanted too. You've riled up a hornet's nest in Harlan's Watch that I suspect I'll be dealing with for years."

"Sorry," I said.

"I'll add it to the charges." With that Chief Constable Nahrman stood and walked to the door. He paused but did not turn back around. "Thank you, you've made this town a safer place." Then he walked out, and I heard the door lock behind me.

13

Harlan's Watch had experienced nothing like that day. It was like the OJ Simpson white Bronco chase had taken him to the crucifixion from *Passion of the Christ*, without all the blood and religious persecution. Okay, maybe that was a crappy analogy, but give me a break, I was tired and about to die.

The entire town watched my perp walk up to the hill. I squinted into the harsh sun and towards the freshly erected gallows atop the hill across the bridge. I really wished I could have raised my arms to block the sun, but my hands were tied behind my back. After all, I was a murderer. A tomato splatted against the side of my head and provided some relief from the brightness. There seemed to be a real difference of opinion about me in town. Some of the gawkers howled in rage while others cheered and gave me hearty thumbs up.

The Chief Constable had told me that I'd really riled people up. I'd exposed the local crime syndicate, which made Master Grimslee and his patrons on the town council none too happy. I suspected that many of the ne'er-do-wells that were pummeling me with foodstuffs were either paid by them or had found their ill-gotten wealth suddenly diminished. However, most of the victims of their extortion were among my fans. And I smiled at them with genuine thanks. You'd be surprised how much a warm and genuine smile helps when you're facing imminent death.

I wore the same rags they'd given me when I'd been booked. I'd asked for my priestly robes back, but the Mayor had said I'd debased the name of my god and was therefore no longer worthy of my title. He didn't seem to care that my god was dead, and he berated me with moralistic furor. That he was facing a tribunal for his partnership with Grimslee didn't seem to strike him as hypocritical.

The day was hot and I was thirsty as all hell. Several more tomatoes smashed against me, which didn't bother me too much, cuz a bit of their juice dribbled down to my mouth. However, the rock that smashed me in the eye and caused me to bleed did annoy me.

"Enough of that," I heard Chief Constable Nahrman say and then he was by my side, shielding me from further harm with his terrible glare. "He's already facing the gallows, leave him what dignity he has." Another rock hit me in the face and Nahrman snapped a finger and pointed at the culprit. One of his deputies walked up and pushed the man back. Then I felt a firm, but gentle hand on my back, guiding me across the bridge where I'd died so many times.

The Chief Constable leaned in close and whispered in my ear. "You're planning to escape."

I nearly stumbled, but the constable's iron grip held me upright. My eyes flashed up to him and I knew his words were not a question, but a statement of fact. I knew those eyes would suss out any lie I could put forth, so I did the only thing I could and nodded.

"I see now. You want me to bring you to the hill which just so happens to be outside the sphere of old Harlan's negation field."

My eyes widened, and I knew I'd given it away. Chief Constable Nahrman grinned at me. "Dammit," I said under my breath.

"So, either you have a port stone, or you have an accomplice who can port you out of here."

"Yes," I said and hung my head low. *I'm sorry Gryph, I've failed you.* I'd come this far, lived through a thousand deaths, and killed innumerable people, just to fail. Unbidden tears came to my eyes, and I felt like every perp at the end of a *Law & Order* episode, broken, beaten and ready to spill my guts in a dramatic confession scene.

The Chief Constable stared at me, but I'd used up all my smartass quips or witty comebacks.

"You have earned the wrath of some powerful people, and I do not mean the rabble that runs Harlan's Watch. You have earned the ire of the Pantheon, of the High God Aluran himself."

I stopped and looked down at the ground at my feet. "So, it's back to the cell then?"

For several long moments, the Chief Constable just looked at me. The sound of the burbling river that had so often been the harbinger of my imminent death now calmed me. I could feel the mood of the crowd grow from excitement to confusion. Finally, the Chief constable leaned in close.

"Many people around these parts do not hold faith with the Pantheon," he said, and my eyes snapped up to his. "Many of us have seen the misdeeds done in the name of false gods.

Some of us have even been on the butt-end of their spears. Some of us have fared even worse." He looked at me and smiled. "I will get you to the hill. I just hope you really do have a way out of the hangman's noose."

"Thank you," I said.

He shoved me rather hard, but I checked my anger, realizing that he had to keep up appearances. The last several hundred yards felt like an instant eternity as time sped up and dragged.

Maybe I have gone crazy.

But, eventually I stood on the gallows. The Mayor stepped forward and read the charges against me, but I didn't listen. Then the noose slipped over my head and around my neck. The crowd grew silent, and I felt the cloth of the hangman's hood brush against my ear.

"Hey Pal," the hooded hangman said low and for my ears only.

"Vonn?" I said in shock.

"Indeed. I knocked the hangman out and stole his hood. It was kind of a hoot."

"Oh man, you became Enrico Pallazzo for me," I said, with utter joy. "You're the best."

"I have no idea who that is."

"Yeah, few people do, but those who get it are giggling right now."

"I'm here to free you."

"No need, my friend. I got it covered. But stay close."

I could almost feel Vonn's grin. "You have the Agent's port stone," he said.

He was right, and at that very moment the magic pebble that was my salvation was in a death grip in my right hand. It had been there ever since the execution squad had come for me. Up to that point I'd hidden it in my beard. Yup, just like the poison and the bit of sausage roll from oh so long ago. How strange that my very life relied on a quirk of fate and an unruly beard.

Had I not sunk so low and eaten that crumb of forgotten yumminess, I might never have discovered what every bearded man took for granted; beards were treasure troves of hidden delights.

After killing the Agent, I'd scrambled for the port stone. Sure, I wanted to burn the *Warrant* and steal all her swag. Until that disappointing moment, I had no idea that she was a Player. That had pissed me off. I had worked my ass off and felt I deserved her gear. But, under the circumstances I was happy with the port stone and the continued living it would buy me. Besides, her slinky armor would not have done my figure justice.

So, just before the constables came, I stashed the marble sized miracle in my beard, and every few minutes thereafter, I'd obsessively checked to see if it was still there. Everyone, including Chief Constable Nahrman just assumed I was a pretentious bearded hipster, over-proud that the genes I had no influence upon had given me decent facial hair.

Then it was a waiting game. The Chief Constable and I got to know each other and became better buds than I ever dreamed was possible. All the while I kept using *Player Tracker*. It kept giving me an ERROR message, which was the real reason behind my deepening depression.

But then, happy day, just around the time the Chief Constable realized I was an NPC, I felt Gryph. I knew where he was. All I needed to do was get beyond the negation field and port back to my good buddy. Then I'd punch him in the mouth for putting me through all this shit. We have a complicated relationship.

The Mayor was finishing his speech and turned to me. "Does the condemned have any last words?"

"I do." I cleared my throat in an overly dramatic and obnoxious fashion. This went on for several seconds before the Mayor's irritation boiled over and he snapped at me to get on with it. "There are no perfect men nor many perfect women. I am not a perfect man, nor a... Umm... perfect woman, but I have tried to live my life by the ideals I believe in.

Sure, sometimes those ideals have led me to unfortunate incidents of mass murder, and maybe, just maybe, occasionally, I liked the killing, but I ask, does that make one a bad person?"

Numerous nods and several confused mumbles of "yes" filled the crowd, even from some of those who had, until then, been really supportive.

This isn't going quite the way I'd hoped.

"Anyway, my point is, that we all try to do the best that we can in this life. That, I guess, is my message to all of you fine folks gathered here today." I paused, and aside from the occasional cough, the crowd looked at me with confused silence.

"Okay, anyway, that's about all I have to say today, apart from this. Kids, say no to drugs, just do it and, uh, stay in school." I looked right at the Mayor and grinned. He scowled throu his thin lips and his weasel eyes glared judgment.

"Catch ya on the flip side," I said, and I sent a mental command to the port stone.

I felt Vonn grab me a bit too tightly, like a girlfriend really turned on by a ride on her hunky boyfriend's new motorcycle. I only had a moment to feel uncomfortable however before the world turned inside out. Light expanded and contracted in concert. Up became down, left became right and then we shifted, and we were somewhere else. I fell to my knees and the thin gruel and rock-hard bread they'd fed me in the pokey came back up.

"You okay," I heard Vonn say. I waved my hand back at him in annoyance.

Why does everyone else seem immune to that shit?

At least this time I was on some soft grass. After a minute I regained my composure and stood. Vonn handed me a water skin. I drank heartily and then passed it back to him.

"Thanks," I said. "For everything."

He nodded and then pointed at my face. "You got a little something in your beard there."

I reached up to find my beard had not survived my retching unscathed. Bits of partially digested muck crusted my thick facial hair. "Uggh, I need to shave this thing off."

Vonn handed me a satchel that looked remarkably like my own. I opened it to find all my gear. My eyes snapped up and he answered me before the question even formed on my lips.

"I told you I was more rogue than knight. While everyone was all distracted with the mass arrests and your interrogation, I took some liberties with the town evidence locker. Got me some good stuff too."

I jumped at the man and gave him a huge hug. "You're my second-best friend in all the Realms," I said, struggling to hold back a sniffle. "Of course, that may have something to do with the fact that I've killed almost everyone I know a few times too many."

"Yeah, you should probably leave that habit in the past."

I grinned, suited up and had a look around. We were in a valley, between a few tall peaks. Up ahead was an ancient looking tower. It was circular and made of more metal than stone. Around its base was a mound of dirt and grass that resembled the opened peels of a banana as if the tower had recently pushed up from under the earth.

"That's Thalmiir architecture," I said in a stunned tone.

"Is that important?" Vonn said.

"The Thalmiir have been extinct for centuries, and their cities were all lost."

"How do you know that?"

"I don't know," I said, which genuinely concerned me. "Gryph, what have you got yourself into?"

With nothing else to do, Vonn and I walked towards the doorway into the tower. I knew that my Player was somewhere in this ancient lost city, and he needed me.

The End of Killing Time.
Book Three of the Realms.

The Realms will Continue with Scourge of Souls.
Book Four of The Realms.

Turn the page for a Bonus.

Dead Must Die
A Novella of the Realms

Dead Must Die

A Short Novella of the Realms

by

C.M. Carney

Dead Must Die – A Short Novella of The Realms by C.M. Carney

www.cmcarneywrites.com

© 2018 C.M. Carney

Dedication

To my sister, Melissa Luedke.

Just so you have to read a dorky book.

Love Ya Sis!

1

Simon stared at the Barrow King's throne for several long minutes as the conflicting feelings of anger and pride battled within him. It was a chair made from fused bones, which seemed perfect for an undead sorcerer whose real body had died millennia ago, but Simon wasn't sure it was him. Of course, these days he wasn't sure what *'him'* was.

Was he the eons dead boy who'd been tortured and murdered? Was he the eternal spirit in the shape of that boy who'd been an enslaved butler to the Barrow King? Was he the newly minted master of the Barrow? Was he all of those things? None of them?

He would have frowned if he'd had lips or muscles or any flesh at all. But he did not. Simon was undead, and all he had for a body was a cruddy old skull with several missing teeth. Some part of him that wasn't him dredged up the term redneck. The word was foreign, otherworldly, and he wasn't sure how he understood the word or why it made him feel so bad about himself.

Simon turned towards the nearest dread knight. The spectral energies and mists of his body turned with him and he raised a skeletal hand that had not, until that moment, existed and pointed at his undead minion.

"You, come here," Simon said appalled to hear a slight pubescent crack in his voice. He had no teenage male body, so why did he have teenage male problems? *Some sort of residual body image, perhaps?* Simon thought.

The dread knight shambled up to Simon. A part of him knew he should be afraid as the undead beastie came closer, but he was not. He was the master of this dungeon, and the dread knights were his servants. The undead warrior came close, but instead of stopping a polite distance from Simon, the ghoul kept coming until it stood a mere inch from Simon's face. *No respect for personal space, apparently,* Simon thought.

Simon took a step back and the dread knight took a corresponding step forward. He repeated the exercise several times, each with the same result. Finally, Simon grew annoyed and held his hand against his dimwitted servant's chest, arresting his advance.

"Stop. Okay, new rule for all of you," Simon said as he looked at the two other dread knights. "Keep a distance of at least three feet from me at all times unless I say otherwise. Understand?"

A chorus of "Nnnngggggggs" filled the room and the dread knight that was all up in his business backed up to exactly three feet.

"I'll take that as a yes," Simon said. He advanced on the dread knight near him and the undead creature took a step back. Simon took another step, and the creature did the same. "You, stop and stand still," Simon said in irritation. *Are these damn idiots going to take everything so literally?*

Simon reached up and to his relief, the dread knight stayed put as Simon gripped the creature's least rotten tooth. With a gentle side-to-side motion, Simon worked the tooth until it came free with a dry tearing sound. He looked at it a moment, cursing the vanity that made him even consider this idea, then shrugged and crammed the tooth into one of the gaps in his own skull. There was a small tug as the tooth slurped up and into the jawbone. *Huh, gross. Wasn't expecting that to work.*

A few minutes later he'd commandeered enough teeth to have a full smile. He had one of the dread knights hold up the shiniest shield it could find and got a decent enough look at his new smile. It wouldn't appear in any pearly white toothpaste TV commercials, but at least he had a full set. *Toothpaste? TV? Commercials? What the hell is wrong with me?* A part of his brain understood these words, but he did not know why. After a moment, typical teenager apathy took hold, and he shrugged, returning his attention to his new teeth.

"Not too shabby," Simon said, irritated that he still heard a slight high-pitched crack in his voice. "Okay, what now?" He looked around. Several corpses, bits of broken bone, rusted pieces of metal and other unidentifiable detritus littered the floor. Simon tried to scowl but found that it was impossible to make a facial expression when one had no face. This further ruined his mood and with an irritated wave of his hand he ordered his minions to clean up the place.

He watched their herky-jerky motions for a time, but soon boredom took over and he plopped himself onto the throne of fused bone with a grumpy sigh. *Hmmm, how can I sigh without lungs?* he thought, but the question had barely formed when a presence surged into his mind as if another consciousness had eased into his own. It startled him so much that he fell off the throne, his skull clattering and his misty body dissipating.

With a grunt of annoyance, Simon willed his skull aloft and reformed his ethereal form. His head sat askew, and he formed a pair of hands to move it back into place. Then he glowered at the throne. "What the hell was that?" he yelled, and his voice echoed around the chamber. None of the dread knights or corpses they piled up against the wall answered.

He sat back down on the throne as hesitantly and gingerly as a man with a bad case of hemorrhoids. For a moment Simon felt nothing, but then the presence returned. It was a slight pressure that slowly built in intensity. Simon wanted to flee but forced himself to remain still. This time the presence eased itself into his mind as if understanding the error, it had made the first time. A chill moved through him, like an intense case of goosebumps and then a voice spoke.

You are not he, the voice said.

"Ahhhh!" Simon squealed, and he nearly fell off the throne again. "What? Who?" he sputtered.

You are not he, the voice repeated.

"I have no idea what you're talking about," Simon said rather more loudly than he meant to.

The lich… Ouzeriuo, the voice said.

"No, I am not Ouzeriuo. I hate that guy."

Hate?

Simon tried to explain the meaning of the word but could not come up with a satisfactory definition. But his mind seethed around the concept and he knew the presence understood.

Hate. Yes. Also hate Ouzeriuo.

"Yeah that guy was a douche," Simon said, wondering

how he knew what the foreign sounding word meant.

Douche?

"Never mind," Simon said and then grumbled when he realized that he was speaking aloud to a voice in his head. *Who are you?*

I... am the Barrow, the voice said in a manner that made Simon wonder if it had never described itself with the pronoun.

The Barrow? I don't understand.

It is... difficult to explain, the voice said, and Simon sensed the presence struggling to find the right words. *I am the sentience that animates this dungeon. Without my presence, it would simply be passageways of rock and haven to monster and beast. Without me, it would be a place of pointless life and wasted death.*

So, you're telling me you're some kinda spirit who possesses the Barrow? Simon said.

No, I am the Barrow. I am a symbiotic life form. I have no physical form of my own. This makes my ability to alter things in the physical world... complicated. I am meant to join with a physical being, a host, a dungeon master.

And you want me to be this dungeon master?

Yes, together we would be greater than we are alone. Together we can make the Barrow great again.

That was when something occurred to him and panic rushed up inside of him like bile.

You merged with Ouzeriuo.

No, he was unwilling to share, to grow. He wished only to dominate. He loved only power and was driven by fear. I fought against him, worked to foil his plans, but he was powerful, and I grew ever weaker. It is a shame he refused to bond.

Simon scowled or tried to. That whole no flesh thing again. *You're telling me that if he'd been willing you would have bonded with him?*

Of course. He was very powerful. Together we could have made...

Made the Barrow great again, yeah I get it. Anger burned inside him. *But he was evil.*

Evil and good are mortal concepts. They do not concern me.

What? Simon sputtered. *Well, they should.*

I am sorry, they do not. However, if it makes you … feel better … my purpose and concerns will change as the bonding grows. What is you, will become me and what I am will become you.

So, I will make you nicer?

Perhaps. The nature of the bonding is hard to predict.

Simon thought on it for a moment. Was this any different from what Ouzeriuo had done to him?

So let me get this straight, you want to merge with me, infect me, make the two of us one?

Yes, the Barrow said with a sense of purpose and finality.

What's in it for me? Simon asked.

Your mind, your very being will be expanded. You will feel what I feel, know what I know. You will have the potential of everlasting life. You could help shape the Realms in ways you cannot conceive of.

That sounds pretty great, Simon had to admit.

It is, but be warned, the bonding will make us one. What affects me will affect you, and what affects you will affect me.

Is the bonding permanent?

Yes, until you die. Then I will lose some of what I was, but after a time I would bond with another.

I thought you said I'd have everlasting life! Simon grumbled in alarm.

I said the potential for everlasting life, but the Realms are a dangerous place and there are a hundred ways for you to die.

Thanks for that happy bit of news, Simon muttered. He felt like a teenager dumped at the prom watching his date making out with the quarterback. He cocked his head to the side as he wondered what the prom was, or for that matter a quarterback.

At least you are not a 'douche'. That should help your survival chances.

Thanks. Simon pondered the idea for many long minutes, wishing that Gryph had been here to advise him. Simon understood very little about being a dungeon master, but he knew as the conqueror of the Barrow, Gryph held some kind of dominion over it. While Simon would be the dungeon master, Gryph was kinda his boss.

Can I make this kind of decision without him?

But then, in typical teenage fashion, Simon realized his

own wisdom and intelligence far surpassed all others and made his decision. *What the hell, let's do this thing.*

The thing is done, the voice of the Barrow said in his mind.

Simon's body moved and his mind expanded. He was everywhere in the Barrow and nowhere. He felt the wyrmynn huddled and afraid. He slowed momentarily over the cast-off soul stuff that comprised the massive black ooze until the psychic pain emanating from the hive-like mind pushed him away.

Next, they spun through the muggy cave the dark dryad and her fungus minions called home. Simon hovered over her presence a bit longer than was polite, but she intrigued him.

You like her, The Barrow said.

"What?" Simon exclaimed, eyes snapping open. "No man, just checking out any potential threats," Simon said aloud.

If you say so.

"Uncool, dude," Simon said, but let it go and closed his eyes, diving again into the Barrow's perception.

He flowed over the empty enclave in the Gray Haven where a company of thieves had once lived. Gryph had made Simon let the men go even though some of their pals had tried to kill him. "Judge a man by his actions, not those of others," Gryph had told him. Simon understood the idea but thought Gryph had been too nice.

I agree, said the Barrow. *I could have fed on them.*

Fed?

Yes, that is how I sustain my existence. I lure adventures and monsters in and then feed on them.

Ewww, that is …

Efficient.

If you say so.

I am hungry.

A pulse of hunger hit Simon. The sensation was so strong, it nearly drove Simon mad, but then he found his courage. *I triumphed over that dick knocker Ouzeriuo. I will not lose myself to a damn hole in the ground.* A moment of panic pulsed through Simon. *Sorry, no offense.*

None taken.

You are more than hungry; you are starving.

Yes, the Barrow said and a status window appeared in

their shared vision.

The Barrow.

Host: Simon.
Current Tier: 1
True Tier: 8
Health: 1,030/86,890.
Status: Starving.

Race: Sentient Dungeon

The Barrow is one of the most ancient sentient dungeons on all Korynn, but years of neglect have left it starving. To return to its former glory, it needs to feed.

Current Level Essence Points: 3.

Explain what I am seeing, Simon asked.

When I feed I absorb the level essence of the creatures. A level 10 warrior will give me 10 Level Essence Points and 100 health. To survive, I need to consume Level Essence Points equal to my True Tier each day. Currently, I require eight per day.

What happens if you don't have enough Level Essence Points? Simon asked, noting that the Barrow only had three.

Then I cannibalize myself at the cost of 10 health per missing *Level Essence Point per day. Every 10,000 points of health earns a new Tier. If I drop below a Tier threshold, then I lose the ability to create higher level monsters and loot, thus making it more difficult to lure quality prey.*

You eat yourself?

If I must.

What happens if you run out of health?

I will go dormant, and an outside force would need to sacrifice 1000 Level Essence Points to awaken me once more. That is why there are so many dormant dungeons across Korynn.

What happens to me if you go dormant?

You will die.

Panic took Simon, and he looked around at the scattered bodies, both the recently alive, like Dirge and his pals, and the desiccated corpses of the twice dead dread knights. *Why didn't you eat them?*

I needed to form a bond to absorb them.

And Ouzeriuo would not bond with you.

No, he would not. As you said he was a ... douche.

Now that we've bonded, can you absorb them?

Yes, I am in the process now.

As Simon watched, the corpses started to melt, and after a few minutes, they had turned into puddles of viscous goo which were then absorbed directly through the stone floor of the Barrow. *Gross, it's like watching someone chew with their mouth open.*

He also sensed the Barrow's reserve of *Level Essence Points* rise to 168 and its health to 2,710. A flush of well-being flowed through the Barrow and into Simon.

Feel better? He asked the sentient dungeon that was now not only his home but also a part of him.

Yes. I am not whole, but I am better.

Well, good then. Simon let himself expand into this new world that was him and was not him. *Let's find us some tasty grub. I hear wyrmynn tastes like chicken.*

2

Erram was one of those idyllic hamlets whose wondrous mountains, lakes and forests drew artists from around Korynn. These artists would then waste their lives and their talents painting the same scene over and over for tourists. Everyone wanted to live there until they did and then they could not wait to leave.

Its populace was mostly of human ancestry, but a vibrant gnomish community and an enclave of hill dwarves also called the town home. The town was also a popular summer destination for the nobles of the Eldarian Dominion, their hangers-on, the hangers-on of the hangers-on and those of nefarious intent who preyed on all the above.

On any given summer day, a varied cast of characters walked the main thoroughfares and skulked through the back alleys of Erram. It was in this town on a fine midweek morning, when no clouds marred the sky, that Bahldreck, a seventh son of a little respected, yet very wealthy, noble family preached the good word.

"And the High God did sayeth that the dead must die and the living shall stay alive, and no true servant of the High God shall consort with the dead, even if by accident while one was very drunk on elderberry wine. He commandeth thee to not let the dead live and to never speak of their goings-on," Bahldreck droned.

It was his soporific tone, which rivaled even the best sleeping potions, that made Bahldreck's sermons so popular with the town's insomniacs. A group of these unfortunate souls currently slumbered in the grass in front of him, their low snores the only response Bahldreck ever got to his long-winded and rambling exhortations against the undead.

Nobody in Erram knew why the living dead rankled the paunchy noble so thoroughly. Sure, nobody liked zombies or skeletons and a rogue revenant could cause havoc if left unchecked, but Bahldreck hated the undead with a passion that most noble-born sons showed only for drink, women and the crushing of serf rebellions.

None of these things interested Bahldreck who spent every evening, rain or shine, preaching from atop the overturned turnip cart that doubled as his pulpit. He read nightly from his gold-embossed copy of *The Testament of the High God*. Many a thief coveted the beautiful book if only with eyes intent on pilfering the book's gold and not for the words of wisdom it contained. It was the most valuable item in Bahldreck's possession, or so he, and nearly everyone else, believed.

"There, do you see it?" came a deep voice from a dapper gentleman named Verreth. He stood with his companions in the shadows of a broad-leafed tree watching Bahldreck the way a spider watches a fly.

"What? The git on the turnip cart?" asked a wiry Aegyptian named Gerryt.

"Yes, and no," said Verreth as if he were talking to a child or a dimwit who'd fallen off a turnip cart too many times. "Not the git, the necklace."

All eyes turned back to Bahldreck as a beam of sunlight hit the preacher in the chest causing the dullest of glints to flash from a gray amulet hanging around his neck on a length of leather twine.

"It look like tin," grumbled Brahk, an overly muscled half-orc. "Brahk like gold better than tin."

"He's right, enough gold covers that book to keep us in beds and drink for a week," said Serraia, a sea elf air mage long ago exiled by her people.

"We're not defacing a holy book for a few coins of gold," Verreth snapped.

"Since when have you been a man of the gods?" Gerryt asked.

"Ever since I saw Aluran in action," Verreth said. "Now I do not believe the superstitions that the High God sees all, but I like being alive and I have no plans of risking his wrath over a few measly coins."

"Brahk am dumber than stable boy been kicked in head

too many times, but even me know no mess with gods." The others nodded at the truth of the ill-spoken statement.

"Then why do we care about him and his stupid tin bauble?" Serraia asked.

"Because he and his tin bauble will help us plunder the Barrow," Verreth said with a grin.

✳ ✳ ✳ ✳ ✳

Bahldreck still had ten minutes left to his normal sermon but the ominous bank of lightning flushed clouds approaching from the mountains, convinced him he'd accomplished his day's work.

He reverently wrapped *The Testament of the High God* in a protective layer of waxed paper and then secured it inside his waterproof satchel. He climbed down from his pulpit, looking around for any folks who could aid him in turning over his cart so he could be on his way. All nearby eyes quickly found interesting things to look at in every direction save Bahldreck's. Normally he'd corral several of his flock to aid him, but they were slumbering so peacefully at his feet he hated to wake them.

"A sign that my sermon touched their hearts, I'd say," Bahldreck said in a satisfied voice. "Still, waking them to aid me would still be the High God's work, would it not?"

He was about to kick the nearest slumbering man when a honeyed voice spoke behind him.

"May we humble sinners be of service your holiness?"

Bahldreck turned as an odd group of four individuals walked up. The man who had spoken kneeled as Bahldreck turned to them. The other three stood, clearly transfixed by Bahldreck's holy aura, until the other man dragged them off their feet into a proper bow.

He guessed by their dress and demeanor they were humble supplicants, perhaps pilgrims en-route from the southern coast to the Shining City of the High God himself. Bahldreck smiled and bid them to rise.

"We will, but first may we humble pilgrims bask in your holy light for the merest of moments?" asked the man who had spoken.

The sea elf maiden cast a sharp glance at the speaker in a manner that suggested to Bahldreck that she felt unworthy of such an honor. Bahldreck was quick to speak, hoping to reassure her that she, that all of them, were more than worthy to kneel at his feet.

"Well, I don't see why not," Bahldreck said. "After all, that is the proper form."

The four hung their heads low. After several moments the silence unnerved Bahldreck and he begged them to return to their feet. Introductions followed and the massive barbarian Brahk shocked Bahldreck with the ease he turned the cart over. The Aegyptian hitched his pony while the sea elf maiden brushed dirt from his robes. Unnerved by all the attention, Bahldreck mounted his cart and opened his mouth to say his goodbyes, when their leader, Verreth, spoke up.

"Your holiness, may I beg a word?"

"I suppose," Bahldreck said in an uncomfortable tone, hands set to snap the reins.

"We beg your help. I was once a Knight of the Order of the Blazing Fist, but alas I committed a sin and have fallen from the graces of the High God Aluran."

"Alas, that does happen on occasion. Good luck finding redemption." Bahldreck went to snap the reins when the fallen knight knelt once more, right in front of his pony, preventing him from leaving.

"The High God has given me one last chance to redeem myself in his eyes. We all have."

Verreth turned to the others, hands vigorously suggesting that they too kneel. After a moment they did, but Bahldreck was sure he heard grumbling. *The High God will always be heard, even through the most stubborn of ears*, Bahldreck thought, wondering if that was an actual passage from the Testament or just a nugget of deep wisdom from within Bahldreck himself.

"I have seen a vision, sent by the High God himself. He tells me that only by serving you in your great mission to rid the world of the undead, can I hope to regain his favor and have any hope of basking in his light in the afterlife.

"He mentioned me by name?" Bahldreck asked.

The thin Aegyptian Gerryt brought his hand to his mouth, overcome by a coughing fit. Bahldreck was about to order Verreth to assist the man when a discharge of electricity thrummed from Serraia's finger and into Gerryt's side. He yelped and his coughing fit ended. He turned towards her in surprise. Bahldreck could not see the man's face, but he was sure he was thanking the sea elf maiden for casting whatever healing magic had aided him.

Perhaps these folk deserve my esteemed help, after all, Bahldreck thought.

"Yes, my most holy lord. I heard your name from his lips direct to my humble ears," Verreth said, bowing lower. "The High God knows the toils and troubles you've been the victim of and he has sent my compatriots and I to aid you on your great quest."

"Well, yes. It has been a bit of a rough go of late, but I held faith that I deserved better and knew the High God would not disappoint me."

An odd chortling sound came from the barbarian Brahk and Verreth grabbed him by the back of his head and pushed his face hard into the ground. Brahk grunted and mumbled incoherently, but Verreth looked at Bahldreck with a winning smile. "My apologies for this emotional display of devotion. Brahk has lived a wretched life, one marred by violence and sin. Bearing witness to the holy fire contained within your sanctified body has overwhelmed him and turned him away from the path of damnation."

"Well, all men experience the rapturous glory in different ways. I am glad that my body has inspired him."

A shriek of joyous laughter exploded from Serraia's mouth and she quickly covered it with one hand, perhaps embarrassed by her emotional outburst. She buried her head in Verreth's shoulder and beat her fists upon his chest and arms, unable to control her emotions.

"Let it out sister, for the High God has said that joyous outbursts are a celebration of life. I am glad he has found his way to you through me."

"Yes, you ...." Verreth said, his face distorting into a rictus of barely restrained joy. His shoulders shook with the effort and he tried to hold back his tears. He turned away, and Bahldreck was gracious enough to let him recover himself. When he could, he spoke again. "Finding you has been one of the most moving moments of my life, of all our lives. I believe destiny has great plans for us."

"Oh, I am sure, yes. That makes quite a bit of sense," Bahldreck said. A warning alarm flared deep in his mind, but as he often did, he ignored it. "What plans?"

"Well, as it so happens your holiness I have a map given by another servant of the High God. This holy servant suggested that you would know how best to use it in the High God's service," Verreth said and pulled a roll of parchment from his bag and handed it to Bahldreck.

Bahldreck unfurled the scroll to find a map written in some unintelligible script. The land it depicted was familiar, yet foreign. "Hmm," Bahldreck said, a hand cupping his chin in deep thought. "Most interesting and ancient and very pretty and great, you don't know how great."

Verreth walked up and grabbed the map and rotated it a half turn counterclockwise. It was then as the familiar environs of Erram and its surroundings came into focus that Bahldreck realized that he had been holding the map upside down. "Oh yes, I see now. I was just trying to … ummm …"

"Gain a better perspective?" Verreth suggested.

"Yes, exactly. I prefer to look at a problem from all angles."

"I wish I had thought to do the same," Verreth said. "But then that is why you are you and, alas, I am merely me." He turned his intense gaze upon his companions.

Serraia's eyes went wide for a moment and then she nodded. "Oh, yes, very wise indeed," Serraia said. "Well done your holiness."

"It was quite the insight," Gerryt agreed.

Verreth elbowed Brahk whose focus had been on a passing food cart. He turned in a panic to see Bahldreck looking at him expectantly. "Yeah, that stuff they done said. All good and true and junk."

"Yes, well, very good," Bahldreck said and returned his attention to the map. Verreth walked up and placed a gentle hand on the map.

"If you would honor me your holiness, I believe it would be less taxing on you if I were to hold on to the map." Verreth tugged the map from the preacher, rolled it and returned it to his pack. "After all, you have enough to worry about with the plan."

"The plan?" Bahldreck asked in a voice a few octaves higher than was normal. "Ah, of course. I will work diligently and unceasingly on the plan. Plan, plan, planning the plan."

"If you please, your holiness, it would humble me to explain your wondrous plan, as created by you, and explained to me by the High God to our most cretinous companions. There is no need to waste any more of your precious time repeating it to such low types such as these." Verreth indicated the others with a wave of his hand.

"Hey," Gerryt complained, before an elbow from Serraia reminded him of his proper place.

"Yes, of course," Bahldreck said. "That goes without saying. It would be best for you to tell the others of my great and amazing plan. I fear that oft times, my noble manner of speaking can confuse people of your … ummm … ilk."

"Very wise your holiness," Verreth said. "I will remove our unworthy souls from your presence and give you leave."

"Yes, that would be for the best."

"Until tomorrow then, when we journey to the Barrow and assail the vilest of the lords of undeath."

"Until then … wait what?"

3

Verreth and his crew left the idiot Bahldreck standing in the middle of the road, mouth agape like a slack-jawed yokel. They kept up the game of humble supplicants until they rounded a corner.

"You can't be serious," Serraia said. "This guy will help us defeat the Barrow King?"

"Yup," Verreth said with a grin and eased his head around the corner to make sure he didn't lose sight of Bahldreck.

"What, do you plan on throwing him at the Barrow King?" Gerryt asked.

"Not sure that work. Preacher am be dumb, so head probably very hard like Brahk's, but me not sure that would be enough to kill dead lord."

"You mentioned that tin amulet earlier," Serraia said, eyeing Verreth. "You know something about it, don't you?"

"I do," Verreth said with a smug look.

"Want to share with the rest of us?" Gerryt asked.

"Nope."

"That no um seem fair," Brahk muttered.

"It isn't, which is why I'm the boss and you're the underlings."

Gerryt walked up to him and with a flick of his wrist had a dagger pointed at Verreth's jugular. "Why don't we kill you, take that fancy map in your bag and go it without you?"

"For several reasons. One, you have no idea what the amulet does. I do. Two, the map is a fake, a pretty prop I had made up to impress that idiot. Three, the real location of the Barrow is in here." Verreth tapped his head. "And last I checked none of you lot is a thought mage."

Serraia eased Gerryt's knife away from Verreth's throat. "How do you even know the Barrow exists?"

"Yeah. How? I've never heard of it, and I know these parts better than most."

"Because it only recently moved into the neighborhood."

"What?" Gerryt asked.

"Yeah, what?" Brahk agreed. "Dungeons no move. Ain't got no legs."

"Trust me it moved, and I know where."

"Again, how?" Serraia asked, impatient.

"Let's just say I overheard a drunk gnome with an irritating imp bragging about it. They were heading there the next morning. So when he passed out, I pilfered his map, memorized it and gave it back."

"Why'd you do that? He could end up getting the treasure." Gerryt whined.

"That's not how dungeons work. They generate monsters and treasure to lure adventurers in. They're like those plants that create sticky sap to lure flies." Verreth paused until his companions had all nodded in understanding. "Some adventurers get killed and the dungeon feeds upon them, using the energy to sustain itself and spawn new monsters. Then, the process begins anew.

"So even if the gnome and his buddies survived, the Barrow will have regenerated by now," Serraia said.

"Yes," Verreth said with a smile. "But they are likely all dead. They were way underpowered to handle the Barrow."

"And we're not?" Gerryt asked.

"We are, but Bahldreck or more accurately Bahldreck and that amulet are more than a match for the Barrow."

"You sure about this?" Serraia asked.

"I am," Verreth said.

A tense silence fell across the group until Gerryt spoke up. "Okay, I'll play along, for now."

Verreth looked at the others, who both nodded. "Good, for now, we need to keep an eye on him. He'll try to flee once his pea-sized brain realizes what he's gotten himself into. So Gerryt, you track him, find out what inn he's staying at and send word to us."

"Why me?" Gerryt asked.

"Because you're the best tracker we have and as payment for your grievous and unprovoked assault on my personage. Be happy I'm the forgiving type."

"What do we do when Gerryt finds the inn his holiness is

holed up in?" Serraia asked.

"We find a nice woman to liquor him up and keep him company until we leave tomorrow."

Brahk looked at Serraia, who flushed in anger.

"No not her you idiot," Verreth said. "He already knows her, and she's not that nice."

"Up yours Verreth," Serraia said.

"Ha, ha, Verreth is right, you a bitch Serraia," Brahk said, laughing like a dying cow.

"I will shank you, orc."

"And prove you bitch? Ha." Brahk chortled happily to himself.

"I'll catch up with you guys later," Verreth said, pulling up his hood. "Do not lose him."

"Where are you going?" Gerryt asked.

"There's one more part of this plan I need to arrange." Verreth rounded a corner and vanished into the crowd.

Gerryt sighed and peaked around the corner to see Bahldreck climbing up on his cart. "This had better be worth it," he said and melted into the shadows.

Bahldreck slept on a raft floating on the slowly rolling sea of his mind. It was a peaceful, if dull sea, barely lit and wrapped in a thick fog. Bahldreck felt happy. He was never happy, and he wasn't sure why he was happy now. A voice bubbled through the surface of the sea, a voice from the part of his brain whose job it was to ensure that the happiness did not continue. *Get up you worthless slug.* The voice sounded different to Bahldreck, its tone was harsher and more hostile than his normal self-loathing internal critic. In his mind, Bahldreck waved the irritating voice away.

"Just a few more minutes Mommy," Bahldreck mumbled and rolled onto his side, the raft shifting under his weight. Distant rumbles of thunder rolled over him, but his dulled danger sense failed to sense the coming storm. Then the raft overturned, and his eyes flashed open in time to see the filthy dirt floor his face was about to make friends with.

His face hit the floor hard and one of his teeth bit through his lip. The raft, that was no raft at all but a filthy mattress, landed on top of him cascading him in a cloud of dirt and dust. The copper taste of blood mixed with the sting of dust in his eyes combined to drag his mind to alertness.

"By Ganneth," the preacher barked in alarm, and pain surged through his head. Other sensations followed. A foul, mucky paste soured his parched mouth, bitter nausea roiled his stomach and the wet patch on the crotch of his robes started to furiously itch.

"What?" was all he said before a pair of none too gentle hands lifted him up and sat him on a rickety chair near the overturned bed. He forced his eyes to focus and saw a large half-orc staring down on him. The massive green tinged man was scowling at Bahldreck, but whether it was from the preacher's current state or the orc's natural disposition Bahldreck couldn't say.

"I don't have any money," Bahldreck said in a panic.

"What, just cuz me am half-orc mean me thief?" the half-orc, who Bahldreck now remembered was named Brahk, said in an offended tone.

Bahldreck just stared, his bladder threatening to further foul his robes. "Ummmm ...."

"Ha, Brahk kidding. You broke. Brahk already search you when passed out." The half-orc slapped Bahldreck on the back and then grimaced. He brought his hand to his nose and sniffed. "Eww, you be gross."

"Ummmm ... What is happening?"

"Verreth says time to go, so we go. Time to go Barrow kill undead."

"The Barrow?" Bahldreck said and then a slew of memories from the previous evening came rushing back in a disjointed mishmash. He remembered meeting up with Verreth and his admiring pals and celebrating his continuing battle against the undead with a very nice lady the previous evening. Downing many, many pints of ale, and then several rounds of a potent liquor called Jayger Meister concocted long ago by a legendary player. But amidst all of this one memory was the most potent. "The Barrow?" Bahldreck sputtered again and a tremble from deep in his bowels threatened to add further stains to his robes. "Yeah, I don't think today is the best day."

"No care. Get up," Brahk said.

Sometime later, after acquiring clean robes and adding the previous night's exorbitant tab to his father's line of credit, Bahldreck emerged into the warm early morning sun and joined a crusade against the dead.

Several hours passed as they followed Verreth through the foothills and up into the mountains. They encountered little resistance, and at noon they stopped for lunch in a small glade near the entrance to a well-hidden mountain pass that Verreth assured them led to the Barrow.

Gerryt had snared several rabbits and Bahldreck's stomach growled as the Aegyptian passed the steaming spits around. His hangover had made eating that morning impossible, and he was halfway through the first rabbit when the stealthy hunter spoke up. "Save some for the rest of us you greedy bastard."

Bahldreck looked up at the man in bewilderment. Surely, he did not expect a man of his breeding and class to subsist on a single rabbit. It was a well-known fact that the common folk required less food to sustain their thin frames and ill health. Conversely, it took quite a bit of food to sustain Bahldreck's own round physique. *It was high time that someone educate these common folk the way of the world*, Bahldreck thought. It was clear from the foreigner's grim stare he needed that lesson sooner than others.

"Leave him be Gerryt," Verreth said. "His holiness will need his strength."

"Thank you Verreth," Bahldreck said, sucking the last bits

of greasy meat from the rabbit's leg bone before tossing it over his head. "Perchance, is there any more rabbit?"

Serraia gripped Gerryt's arm preventing the hunter from leaping over the fire. "Now, now Gerryt, listen to Verreth, his holiness needs his strength if he is to stand at the head of our party and hold the undead at bay."

"Front? Undead? At Bay?" Bahldreck sputtered and his full stomach was suddenly a lot less satisfying.

"You do know that's why you're here, right?" Serraia said in the same tone Bahldreck's father used when explaining obvious concepts to his serfs, employees and, now that Bahldreck thought about it, to him as well. "You're a consecrated priest of the High God Aluran. Who is better equipped to use the holy fire within them to push back the plague of undead on Korynn than you?"

Unease flowed through Bahldreck, and it took several moments for him to understand its source. "Yeah, about that. I'm not sure I'm actually, formally, according to the official priests of the High God Aluran, technically a priest."

"What the hell does that mean?" Gerryt sputtered. "You're not consecrated?"

"Oh, no I am," Bahldreck said, the nervous twinge in his voice causing it to rise several octaves. "I was initiated into the Holy Order of the Turnip by my father's cook. Or was it the gardener?"

"Turnip?" Serraia asked, her voice nearly as alarmed as Gerryt's.

"Brahk no like turnips."

"Yeah, not really the thing to get hung up on big guy," Serraia said. She turned to Verreth. "Did you know about this?"

"No, but it doesn't matter."

"What do you mean it doesn't matter?" Gerryt spat.

"I have faith in a power greater than all of us, and it is very, very close to our friend here," Verreth said, idly stroking at his neck as if he were wearing a necklace or an amulet. "Very close."

"Okay, I'm gonna need more than that," Serraia said.

Verreth smiled and looked up. The sun dipped behind the mountains and ominous shadows crept over the glade. "I think you'll be getting your "more" any minute now."

Serraia and Gerryt looked around suspicious. Brahk retrieved the discarded rabbit bones and chomped them, each echoing crunch causing Bahldreck to twitch or jump.

Bahldreck stared nervously at his hands. Hands that had never seen an actual day's work in their life. *I'm not cut out for this,* he thought and had it been said aloud, anyone who'd ever set eyes on him would have heartily agreed with the sentiment.

He strained his mind to find a way out of his predicament. He'd never been on an actual adventure. In fact, he'd never been anywhere except the family estate and Erram and the road between the two. He told the others as much, and upon getting no response, he looked up to discover he was alone in the glade, and a half dozen rotting corpses were shambling towards him.

4

A squeal tore through the air, echoing back and forth along the thin mountain pass where it heightened in volume and intensity. Had there been any knights-errant wandering the wilderness, they would have been compelled to seek the source of the scream, expecting to find a damsel in distress in need of saving. Alas, it would greatly disappoint them to discover that said maiden was in truth a portly middle-aged twit.

Unfortunately for the not quite consecrated priest of the High God, there were no knights about, just the group of pilgrims he'd entered the glade with, and they were hiding behind a nearby outcropping.

"Are those zombies?" Gerryt asked.

"Actors," Verreth replied casually and took a sip from a wineskin before passing it to the hunter.

"Ha!" Serraia exclaimed before clapping a hand over her mouth. "That was the other part of the plan you were setting up?"

"Yup," Verreth said with a grin as Bahldreck tried to stand, tripped over his robes and nearly fell into the fire.

"Nnngghh. Rarrghh. Groowwwll!" the various zombies said, arms held stiffly before them as they ambled closer to the panicked preacher.

"No very good actors," Brahk said before upending the wineskin and squeezing a jet of wine into his open mouth.

"True enough, but they work cheap," Verreth said.

"Okay, I get it, this is hilarious. But how in the Abyss does it help us fight the Barrow King?" Serraia asked.

"Watch, and learn," Verreth said with a grin, grabbing the wineskin from Brahk and taking a deep drink.

The actor zombies believed they had been hired by Bahldreck's father to teach the boy a lesson in bravery, honor, and manliness. If they succeeded, they were promised further contracts. Seeing Bahldreck scream and flounder in the dirt, not one thespian in the group expected to earn those contracts.

They'd been told to scare the lad as much as possible without getting close enough for him to see through their shabby costumes. That order was proving difficult to achieve, as none of them had ever seen someone so ineffective at fleeing, or even standing upright for more than a few seconds. Perhaps that was why they failed to notice the tin amulet at Bahldreck's neck had started glowing, dimly at first, and then slowly brighter.

"By the nine winds, what is that?" Serraia asked.

"That is salvation," Verreth said.

The actor zombies saw the strange glow and a creeping fear crawled up their spines. They abandoned the zombie part of the act and gave each other nervous glances.

Bahldreck had regained his feet and was now shaking like a man wracked in the throes of an epileptic seizure. His eyes rolled back into his head and he turned towards the sky to scream. This time the scream was deep, manly and very, very angry.

"Gerrold," one zombie said. "I've got a bad feeling about this."

"As do I Percy, but we are professional actors and we do not abandon a performance because of fear."

"Since when?" Percy asked.

"I worked hard on this script. Let us at least finish the scene."

"Wait, you wrote a script for this?" Percy asked, but no answer came as all eyes in the glade flashed to the preacher.

Bahldreck fell forward and his entire body shook and morphed. Shining golden light exploded from his mouth and eyes and beneath his robes as he grew and expanded.

"I suggest a compromise, Gerrold. How about we finish the scene way over there?" Percy exclaimed. "It has been some time since we have practiced fleeing with dignity."

"Huzzah, that is an excellent suggestion," the man named Gerrold agreed. He brought his hands to his mouth and in a clear, sing-song voice, yelled, "Run away, run away."

The zombies tried to flee, but it was too late.

The figure that had been Bahldreck stood and had those present not witnessed his transformation with their own eyes, they would never have believed there was any commonality to the two men. Where Bahldreck had been paunchy, pale and fragile, the mountain of a man now standing amidst the shredded remnants of priestly robes was a paragon of masculine virtues.

He wore a battle-scarred suit of plate mail that shimmered with an internal moon blue glow. He stood 6'9" and weighed at least 400 lbs. With a snick of steel on steel, he drew a massive great sword. In any other's hands, the blade would have been a two-handed weapon, but the man swung it in a lazy one-handed arc, bisecting the closest zombie at the waist.

"Dead must die!" the man screamed in a voice that would have scared off a dragon, had there been any dragons left to frighten. He thrust the sword forward into the guts of another zombie

"What in the Abyss?" Serraia asked, panic creeping into her voice.

"That, my friends, is our weapon against the Barrow King," Verreth said with a grin. "Meet Sir Herman Heinrich Humperdinck, or what remains of him."

Sir Humperdinck grabbed another of the zombies by the head and squeezed. The sputtering howl that came from the actor's mouth was horrific but ended abruptly when his skull popped amidst the sound of grinding bone and explosion of blood and brain matter.

"That glow, he's … dead." Gerryt said.

"Yes and has been for centuries," Verreth said. "But, I wouldn't mention that to him."

"Why not?" Gerryt almost squealed.

"Because he doesn't know he's dead. Don't think he'd react too well to the news."

To punctuate that warning Sir Humperdinck tossed the now headless corpse at several of the other zombies with such force it just didn't knock them from their feet, it knocked their feet off of them.

"Brahk never want talk to big shiny man."

"Probably for the best," Verreth agreed. "In life, he was the most fearsome slayer of the living dead ever seen in this realm or any other. He nearly wiped out every undead creature on Korynn, but the Arch Lich Negvaar cursed him and he became a spectre bonded to his own amulet."

"That crappy bit of tin has contained that monster all this time?" Gerryt asked.

"Yes. It was a symbol of his order. They were a humble folk uninterested in wealth or fame. They donated every bit of gold, silver, and copper to charity. All they had left was tin."

"They be a bunch of dumbasses," Brahk said, before ducking behind the outcropping as Sir Humperdinck tore another zombie in half with his bare hands.

"His zealotry is our gain," Verreth said with a smile.

"Wait, why did he come out now? Those poor schmucks aren't undead, just horrible actors," Serraia said.

The rogues hiding behind the bluff searched for signs of guilt on Verreth's face. He simply stared back at them. "Would you feel better if I pretended to be upset about it?" He paused, but nobody spoke. "As expected." He took a deep breath and looked at Brahk. "Remember the remains of the skeleton I had you collect?"

"One haunting crypt in Erram?" the barbarian orc asked. "Yup, Brahk remember."

"Well like all undead those bones give off a low-grade field of death magic. Our mountainous pal there can sense that energy, and when he does he pops out of the amulet and goes on a killing spree."

Blood-curdling screams of terror rose in the glade and then suddenly ended as Sir Humperdinck swung a zombie actor by his ankle into his last compatriot again and again. Both bodies pulped under the force and soon the spectral knight stood alone in the glade.

"You gave each one of them one of those bones, didn't you?" Serraia said in shock.

"Sure did, told them it was part of the costume. Help make it more authentic and such. Once enough of them got close enough to ol' Bahldreck, it was only a matter of time before he turned into Sir Humperdinck."

"You killed them," Serraia said.

"No, I didn't. He did." Verreth pointed at Sir Humperdinck.

180

"And here I thought I was an amoral prick," Gerryt said.

"I said I felt bad about it."

"No you didn't," Serraia said.

"No?" Verreth watched as each one of his companions shook his head no. "Huh, thought I did." With a shrug, Verreth stood, raised his hands above his head and walked towards Sir Herman Heinrich Humperdinck. After a pause Gerryt followed, keeping Verreth between him and the giant knight.

"I will be damned to the Abyss," Serraia muttered to herself and stood as well. She looked back at Brahk who was still cowering behind the outcropping of rock. "Brahk, come on," she said. He shook his head no, and she waved her hand vigorously. After a moment, the half-orc reluctantly got to his feet and followed.

Sir Humperdinck's shoulders moved up and down as he calmed from his blood rage. He looked down at the remains of the zombie in his hand, a part of his mind wondering why so much fresh blood dripped from the leg of the corpse. Before he could dwell too deeply on the matter a voice called out to him.

"Hello, my brave and worthy knight, I beseech thee to let we humble pilgrims aid you in thine quest."

Sir Humperdinck turned to see a gentleman smiling up at him. Behind him walked a thin man dressed in the dark green of a hunter, a charming looking sea elf maiden and a brutish half-orc whose wide eyes showed admiration, or mayhap it was fear.

"Well met pilgrims," Sir Humperdinck said as he wiped the blade of his sword on one of the zombie's cloaks. "I am Sir Herman Heinrich Humperdinck, Seneschal of the Order of the Blazing Fist, hunter of the undead and slayer of necromancers.

Perchance could you tell me where I am? In my holy rage, I seem to have forgotten."

"My name is Verreth, and these are my compatriots. We are near the hamlet of Erram, fine Sir, close to the dread Barrow, the lair of the evil lich known as the Barrow King."

"A lich you say?" Sir Humperdinck spat eyes wide in anger. "They are the foulest of the lords of undeath. Where is this Barrow?"

"Well, Sir Knight, as chance would have it we were en route to that oubliette of horrors. Like you, we are slayers of the undead. We would be glad to guide you if you would deign to spend time in our ignoble company."

Sir Humperdinck eyed the pilgrims, whose garb suggested neither holiness nor humbleness, but he had spent a lot of time in strange and foreign lands and learned that appearances could be deceiving. He stepped forward and shook the man Verreth's hand.

A tickle of doubt built in the back of his mind as his boot sunk into a patch of blood-sodden grass. He looked down at the closest zombie corpse, noting the eyes staring back up at him held the last vestiges of fear. They seemed so fresh and lifelike, apart from the being dead part.

Have the death priests created a new type of zombie? He wondered to himself and began to kneel.

The man named Verreth grabbed him by the forearm, turning Sir Humperdinck's eyes down to him. "Do not worry yourself over the foul remains. My people will tend to them."

"They know the proper cleansing rituals to perform so they will not rise again?"

"Yes, of course," Verreth said and motioned to the half-orc. "Brahk here is an expert on … cleansing. He knows to pour the blessed water he stores in his wineskin upon the corpses."

The half-orc looked from Verreth to Sir Humperdinck to his wineskin and back at Verreth before his eyes widened in understanding and he poured the blessed water onto the corpses. It was redder than Sir Humperdinck remembered, but then Verreth spoke again drawing the knight's attention from the curiosity.

"Serraia will burn the corpses if you would like to discuss

our plans for assaulting the Barrow."

"Burning the undead is no job for such a fine and comely maiden," Sir Humperdinck said affronted.

"You are right of course. I will have Gerryt tend to the task."

"Yes, that sounds much more proper," Sir Humperdinck said, not seeing the scowl Gerryt gave to Verreth over his shoulder.

"And perhaps you would enjoy Serraia's company. A small chat or a neck massage."

The huge knight flushed as the sea elf walked up to him and took him by the arm. He was so charmed by her he missed the angry glare she cast at Verreth.

"While that would be lovely, our time would be better spent journeying to this Barrow. Lichs are ancient and highly intelligent. They are masters of foul magics and though they are despicably evil their long, unnatural lives have gifted them with a perverted wisdom. This master of the Barrow will be cunning. We will need to be more cunning still if we hope to slay it."

5

Deep in the Barrow, the master sat on his throne. His flowing robes of black smoke seemed almost alive in their movements. A spectral hand moved up and formed a fist. The skull that was the only physical component of this new Barrow King plopped onto the fist with an exaggerated annoyance only a teenager could muster. The silver light flickering in the empty eye sockets grew more agitated.

"I am sooooo bored," Simon whined and tossed part of a leg bone at the nearest dread knight, the one he'd ordered to stand on one leg and hop up and down. His aim was true but the desiccated corpse didn't even notice as the bone bounced off its face.

He held out his free hand and the reanimated corpse of the man named Dirge handed him another bone. "We could engage in some witty repartee, master."

Simon tossed the bone at another dread knight. This one was rubbing its stomach in a circular motion with its right hand while patting the top of its head in time with its left. Again Simon's aim was true, and the bone smacked the undead warrior in the eye, causing it to dangle from its socket. Like his brethren, the dimwitted undead didn't seem to notice.

"No, last time we did that you used a bunch of words I didn't know and it made me feel bad. I want to feel good and do something fun. Maybe I should bury you up to your neck again in the Wyrmynn's latrine."

"I'd rather you not, all things considered," Dirge responded in his silky, almost seductive, voice.

"You're boring too," Simon said and tossed another bone at a third dread knight. This one's arms were splayed wide and had been spinning in circles for the better part of an hour without getting dizzy. The bone's jagged end pierced the corpse's side and stuck. Despite the small victory, Simon refused the next proffered bone.

"Are you still upset the Dark Dryad canceled your date?"

"No," Simon whined. "And she didn't cancel it, she was sick. Some kinda fungal infection. Probably got it from one of those walking blobs of spores she uses as minions."

"Yes, that is a convincing possibility," Dirge said.

Simon's sockets snapped over to Dirge. "What's that supposed to mean?"

"Oh, nothing, just some idle chatter," Dirge said, his voice rising in pitch.

Simon stared at the man. Sometimes he regretted reanimating the Aegyptian assassin. The dude was as unbearable in undeath as he had been in life. *I could just kill him again and reanimate someone else.*

Sadly he didn't have many better options. The Barrow wasn't seeing a great influx of new corpses. Truth be told, he hadn't thought he'd be able to bring Dirge back since the dude's soul had been consumed by a nasty poison. Still living Dirge had tried to use it on Gryph's pal Ovyrm, before the xydai had turned the assassin's own weapon against him.

Dirge had suggested his current charming personality was a biological echo left in his brain after his soul perished. The theory was bolstered by his dispassion concerning the loss of said soul.

Maybe you need to have a soul to miss having a soul? Simon thought before the paradox made his head hurt. *And how can my head hurt? It's just a damn skull.*

"You think she's cheating on me?" Simon asked in a voice tinged with notes of anger and desperation.

"No, no, no, of course not," Dirge said, casually waving his hand to dismiss the idea. "Who could she be seeing? It isn't like this place is rife with eligible bachelors."

"True," Simon said, unconvinced. He was silent for a moment. "Maybe it's the black ooze."

"Maybe what's the black ooze?"

"Ya know, her other fella."

"What? No. First off, the black ooze ain't a fella. It's an acidic entity made from the cast-off remnants of consumed souls. Second … no."

"Yeah," Simon said frumpily. "That Wyrmynn leader Scarface then?"

"She's not seeing anyone else."

"How can you be sure?" Simon asked, his voice cracking and betraying him again.

"Because there is no one else to see," Dirge answered in exaggerated exasperation. "If you're so concerned about it why don't you have the Barrow keep an eye on her?"

"I would never spy on her," Simon said affronted.

"Oh, I see, the Barrow still slumbers."

"Yes," he said testily, then realized what he'd just admitted to. The Barrow was in fact slumbering. The whole dungeon was some kinda living energy entity. To survive it bonded with a sentient being in a mutually beneficial symbiotic relationship. But, the Barrow's last host had been a real dick knocker named Ouzeriuo. Instead of sharing resources, Ouzeriuo had cut the Barrow out, becoming more parasite that host. This had left the Barrow weak and withdrawn. Simon had promised to change all that when he agreed to bond with the Barrow, but without a steady influx of adventurers, the Barrow had precious little life energy to feed upon. The bodies left behind by Gryph had saved the Barrow from going dormant, but it needed more and was unwilling to 'waste it spying on an entity that poses no threat.'

"You could talk to her. Girls like that kinda thing," Dirge said.

"And say what? Back when I was alive I talked to a girl once, and that ended with my britches pulled down and my underclothes pulled over my head courtesy of her older brother. I learned my lesson that day. Girls don't like talking."

"Not sure that's what you should have taken from that."

But Simon was already not listening. "What she needs is a grand romantic gesture from me."

"Not a bad idea. Women like grand romantic gestures. What do you have in mind?"

"Hmmm, I could kill her other boyfriend in some kinda duel. Ya know like guns blazing at high noon. But I'd need a white hat."

"First, there is no other boyfriend. Second, what the hell are you talking about?"

"It's from a movie I think."

"What's a movie?" Dirge asked.

Simon cocked his skull to the side. He wasn't sure what a movie was but felt he should. From time to time he got flashes of memories that were not his own. Movies, proms, letterman jackets, cold mountains in Korea. He remembered things he'd never seen and places he'd never been.

The Barrow had suggested that they were bits of Gryph's memories, or maybe Wick's. After all, Simon had shared time with both men inside Ouzeriuo's weird soul realm. Who knew what kinda cross contamination their minds had experienced. While that made sense, Simon didn't like it and didn't like Dirge questioning him.

"You can shut up now."

"That isn't very friendly," Dirge said, but a blank stare from Simon's skull shut him up.

Simon sighed, an ability he still didn't understand considering he had no actual body. "I'm bored. This place is boring."

"You said that already."

"Shut up you." The words were barely out of Simon's mouth when an odd tickle at the back of his mind told him the Barrow had awoken.

We have company.

Simon leaned forward in his throne. "Really? Who is it?"

Five adventurers. Four are slightly above average in powers and capabilities. Nothing too threatening. The fifth, however, is teeming with a range of magical energies. He is very dangerous.

"Generate a dread knight in the first chamber. I want to talk to these newcomers."

I cannot. After repurchasing the ability to create new dread knights, I am low on energy reserves. I cannot generate a new dread knight at this time.

Simon stroked his chin, annoyed that the Barrow sounded like a legal disclaimer, whatever that was, then stood and walked to Dirge. The reanimated assassin had only a moment to panic before Simon's hands snapped out, grabbed his neck and wrenched his head from his body. The headless corpse slumped to the ground, and the head stared Simon in the face.

"Well that was unfriendly," Dirge said and a moment later the light behind his dead eyes dimmed and his tongue lolled out of his mouth.

Simon dropped the head on top of the corpse. "That should be enough."

Indeed, the Barrow thought. The head and body decomposed into a viscous jelly and soaked into the hard-packed dirt of the floor. The Barrow fed on the life energy Simon had used to reanimate Dirge. *I am ready.*

Simon closed his eyes, which for him meant dimming the lights illuminating his eye sockets. The shrouded robes dissipated and the skull that Simon now called home clattered to the seat of the throne.

The dread knights continued their belly rubbing, hopping and spinning, paying no heed to their master's departure.

6

Verreth crested the hill and pointed down into a shadowy crevasse sunk deep into the base of the mountain pass. "There. The entrance to the Barrow."

The others squinted into the unnatural shade of the fissure that resembled a wound that had exploded from inside the earth. Poking from the heart of the gash was the tip of a ragged black tower. The entrance was the stuff of nightmares, a doorway built into the center of a gaping, skeletal maw.

"Well, that's over the top," Serraia said.

"The fell undead use fear as a weapon," Sir Humperdinck said. "Do not let this petty warning scare you."

On cue a rancid wind picked up, moaning upwards from the depths of the fissure and flowing over the adventurers.

"It seem good warning to Brahk. Maybe we should go home." The half-orc had already turned around when the massive hand of Sir Humperdinck stayed his departure.

"Fear not friend, no paltry undead can pierce my armor or stay my blade." To prove the mightiness of both, Sir Humperdinck drew his sword and smashed the flat of the blade against his breastplate.

"Yeah, but you're the only one with those two things," Gerryt said.

Sir Humperdinck paid the hunter no heed and raised his sword above his head and roared before rushing towards the fanged mouth of the entranceway.

"Just stay behind him and let him do the heavy lifting and the riches of the Barrow will be ours," Verreth said, clapping Brahk on the back and following the giant knight. The others glanced at each other before joining.

Sir Humperdinck ducked under the stalactites hanging like fangs and passed through the threshold. He failed to notice the precipitous drop in temperature, nor the slight change in air pressure. Ahead of him was an obsidian door carved with frescoes of skeletal beings dragging the living to the feet of a throne made of bone. A shadowed figure sat upon the throne, one desiccated hand reaching out to claim its victims.

There was no door handle or other obvious methods of opening the door, so Sir Humperdinck resorted to the age-old method of banging on the door with his mailed fist. The others passed through the field and stood behind them.

"Anyone else cold?" Serraia asked as an unholy chill sunk into her bones.

"Yup, I'm out of here," Gerryt responded, spun around and walked back up the incline. He got a few feet before smashing into an unseen barrier. "What in blazes?" he asked a hand snapping to his nose. It came away bloody.

A moment later Brahk was there pounding ineffectually on the invisible field. Behind them, the creak of ancient, rusted hinges rose and the obsidian door opened.

Without a moment's hesitation, Sir Humperdinck rushed though, his pristine white cloak whipping in the noxious wind that rose from inside the Barrow.

Serraia looked at the door, eyes wide, before turning around and joining the others in bashing the magical shield.

"It won't work," Verreth said. "We are inside the Barrow. We go forward or we die."

"You knew this would happen, you damn cockalorum," Serraia spat and slapped him.

"Yes, I did," Verreth said rubbing his reddening cheek. "As would you, if you'd ever read anything about sentient dungeons. Now quit your bitching and let's get on with it." He turned and entered the Barrow. A few moments later the others followed.

As soon as the last adventurer was though, the obsidian door slammed shut with a clang of dramatic finality.

*****

Every step Sir Humperdinck took into the Barrow brought him deeper into the vile morass of undeath. He could feel the infernal energies in the stale air, in the rock beneath his feet, in

190

every mote of dust floating around him.

"This place is pure evil," the knight said to his companions.

"Yah think?" the hunter barked, but Sir Humperdinck knew the man was not directing his ire at him. It was born of fear.

"Do not let the fear take hold of you. Therein lies the road to despair and death," Sir Humperdinck said. He held his sword in front of him and the golden glow of holy empyrean magic pulsed forth, pushing both the shadows and the chill back. "Bask in the holy light of my faith and you will find strength."

The hunter muttered a comment disparaging Sir Humperdinck's mother, and her imagined dalliances with goblins, but the knight paid him no heed. He knew sarcasm and humor were signs of a weak will and a lack of faith. Sir Humperdinck's will and faith were as strong as adamantine, and he had never been humorous in all his entire life.

They descended a staircase hewn from the bare rock and emerged into a wide chamber. At the far end was another passage that led further down into the Barrow.

"This seems too easy," Serraia said, a crackling sphere of pale blue formed over her hand and she tossed it across the room. It hovered near the far passageway, giving those without night vision a clearer view of the room.

A low scraping rose, echoing from the passage. It sounded like bones scraping across a piece of slate followed by the sound of sharp metal dragging across the stone. Sir Humperdinck raised his sword, while the others behind him nocked a bow, hefted a mace, drew a thin rapier and summoned blue mystic energy. A moment later a shriveled corpse that had once been a man shuffled into the room.

"Dread knight." Sir Humperdinck said. "It is powerful but brainless and mute."

Tension hung heavy as the creature's dead eyes passed over the group. It raised the rusty sword it had been dragging onto one shoulder, cocked its head and spoke.

"Sup, dudes?" the dread knight said in a voice that was a lot less dry and dead and a lot more cracking and pubescent. "And milady?"

"Uh, what?" Gerryt said.

"Pay the abomination no heed, able hunter. It is a cretinous worm-riddled thing," Sir Humperdinck said.

"I am not worm-riddled," the dread knight said, looking at itself. "This body hasn't been animated long enough to attract any."

"So you admit it, you are a defiled corpse raised for ill purposes too horrible to conceive," Sir Humperdinck said, jabbing his huge sword at the dread knight with all the effort of a man talking with his fork.

"More of a floating skull in a halo of dark smoke," the dread knight said, and then looked at its own body. "Oh, you mean this. Well kinda, I used Dirge's life energy to make it, so not sure if that falls into your 'defiled corpse' category or not." This last bit the dread knight said while holding the first two fingers on each hand up and pulling them down. The gesture was foreign to the adventurers, but its meaning was clear.

"So you admit it. You murdered this Dirge, used his blessed life essence to animate this abomination and thereby damned your soul to the Abyss?" Sir Humperdinck roared.

"I didn't kill him. Ovyrm did, but to be honest, the prick deserved it. And there was nothing blessed about his life, so I doubt there was much blessed about his essence either."

"Corrupter, defiler, heretic," Sir Humperdinck roared and rushed the dread knight. The foul creature had no time to raise its rusted weapon before the glowing two-handed blade sliced clean through its neck. Its head fell to the floor, and the body collapsed in a heap to the sound of dry kindling.

The head rolled around for a few seconds until Sir Humperdinck stepped upon it to arrest its motion.

"What is wrong with you guys? I just wanted to talk."

Sir Humperdinck stepped down hard, crushing the undead beastie's skull into a rotten smear of jelly.

"You sure that was a good idea?" Verreth asked as Sir Humperdinck looked at the muck on his boot with distaste.

The man spun. "It was undead, and I killed it. Is that not why we are here?" The threat of violence should anyone disagree with the monstrous knight was obvious.

"I just meant," Verreth said, hands spread wide in deference. "That knowledge is power, so maybe we should have listened to what it was going to say?"

"Is it me, or did he sound like a whiny teenager?" Serraia asked.

"She means it sounded like her last boyfriend," Gerryt said, elbowing Brahk. The half-orc chortled in amusement.

"I'm serious, but I agree with Verreth. We could have learned something from him."

"It!" Sir Humperdinck roared. "He was an it, and I want to hear nothing more about knowledge. All we need is faith. Facts and knowledge just confuse the mind and lead the soul into temptation."

"Okay then," Serraia said. "You're the boss."

"Yes I am," Sir Humperdinck said with a nod. "Let us be on our way. There are more dead to kill." With that the brawny knight strode down the passageway leaving his compatriots to rush after him.

Behind them the body of the dread knight dissolved and leached into the stone of the Barrow floor like water being absorbed by a parched desert.

7

Deep in the Barrow, the skull that was once the Barrow King shook. A moment later black smoke coalesced about it, raising the skull from the stone seat, forming a robe of wispy darkness. Silvery light sparked from the empty eye sockets and the newly reformed spectre shivered.

"What the hell was that? Asshole! I just wanted to chat." Simon paused waiting for a response. When none came, he looked around searching for Dirge. Then he remembered. "Oh yeah, I killed that dude." Simon sent his thoughts inwards.

That was a Knight of the Blazing Fist, the Barrow said. *A famed order of undead slayers. Though they were all killed long ago.*

"How do you know that?"

Because we killed them.

"Who is we?"

Ouzeriuo and I.

"I thought you two hated each other."

Hate is a mortal emotion. As is love. I did not hate Ouzeriuo any more than I love you. On occasion, we worked together. It is a shame he would not accept a binding with me. He was very powerful.

"You are really shitty at making a dude feel better." The Barrow said nothing. "Oh, so now you're doing the silent treatment?" The silence hung heavier. "So what do we do?" Simon asked, desperate and annoyed.

A Knight of the Blazing Fist is an extremely dangerous enemy to entities such as you and I. They are filled with empyrean light and life magic, powers antithetical to the energies that sustain us. It took the combined might of Ouzeriuo and myself to crush them the last time, and I was much less hungry then.

"So, we're screwed is what you're telling me," Simon said, his voice rising as panic threatened to consume him. "I don't wanna die. I just stopped being sorta dead."

Panic is the province of the weak of mind. We have time and they will need to run the gauntlet through the entire Barrow to reach us.

"Good thinking. They'll never get through the wyrmynn, the black ooze and the garden of the dark dryad without losing some of their people."

And those that fall will strengthen us.

Simon nodded his head and then thought about the dark dryad. "Wait, what about my girlfriend?"

So, she's your girlfriend now? The Barrow said, with a hint of snark. *Good to know.*

Simon scowled again, regretting the lessons in bro on bro insults he'd given the Barrow. "Whatever dude, the point is we can't leave her to get killed by Sir Holy Roller Whackjob."

Technically she is already dead.

"Dude, you know what I mean. You gonna help or not?"

I will help, otherwise I will be alone again and that would be, inconvenient.

"Feeling the love guy. Thanks for that"

You are welcome.

"That was sarcasm dude. If we survive, I'm adding it to the syllabus. Okay then, the first step is riling up the wyrmynn. That cold-blooded bastard Scarface has been a thorn in my side since the day I became the landlord of this place." Simon looked over at the three dread knights who were still engaged in their rubbing, hopping and spinning.

"Yo, Hoppy and … Rubby, you two head to the wyrmynn camp. Get 'em all riled up and lead them towards these invading schmucks and away from my honey bunny's grove. Spinny, you wait until your boys, and hopefully, a bunch of those reptile dickheads are killed and then draw that knight into the black ooze room. If you can avoid getting melted by the ooze, great, if not, it's been nice knowing ya."

All three dread knights turned and hopped, rubbed and spun their way towards the exit. Simon smacked the butt of his spectral hand against his forehead.

"Idiot," he berated himself. "Stop your extracurricular activities and shamble like normal."

The undead warriors stopped and walked from the room. Then Simon closed his eyes and watched events unfold through the Barrow's perceptions.

Sir Humperdinck led the way again. The obnoxious knight kept saying "I've got the lead," every time they went through a door, passed under an archway or crossed any line that could conceivably be a threshold, even though nobody else wanted to take point. They'd faced very little in the way of opposition since dispatching the dread knight, but a constant low-grade field of angst and menace hung over the Barrow. After a few boring hours of wandering in circles, Gerryt offered to point them in the right direction. The knight reluctantly agreed, but only after extracting a promise from Gerryt that he was not taking, nor wanted to take, the lead.

"For a haven of the undead, this place has a surprising amount of life," Gerryt said crumbling a bit of dried wyrmynn dung between his fingers and smelling it. "Wyrmynn and I'd say this is less than a week old." He looked on the ground. "And the fellow who left this rushed after his clutch mates … that way." He pointed down a tunnel that dipped downward.

Sir Humperdinck strode purposefully and noisily down the passage. The other members of the group eyed each other warily, and then one after another followed the blundering knight.

They soon came upon the wyrmynn, or more accurately the wyrmynn came to them. They were chasing two more of the dread knights, and they were hissing mad. A few arrows protruded from the bodies of the dead warriors, the puncturing weapons not very effective against creatures who no longer needed internal organs.

Brahk laughed nervously and pointed at the first of the

undead creatures. An arrow protruded from its crotch, bouncing in a rude phallic manner as the dread knight shambled towards them. Behind it, another dread knight ran, its back a pincushion of a dozen more arrows.

Sir Humperdinck dispatched both beasties with graceful swings of his sword. Then the wyrmynn were on them, lots and lots of wyrmynn. The bipedal lizard men were fierce warriors and by the time the battle was won, a few dozen corpses littered the floor.

One of them belonged to Gerryt.

"Dammit," Serraia said and closed the hunter's eyes. She pulled a necklace from his neck and tied it around her wrist. Verreth and Brahk both comforted her.

"There is no time for sentiment. We need to keep moving," Sir Humperdinck said, impatient.

"Give her a moment," Verreth said in a commanding voice. "They were lovers."

"What do you mean? Sir Humperdinck asked.

Verreth cast a sideways glance of confusion at Brahk.

"What mean what mean?" Brahk asked. "They did it." The knight stared at the half-orc blankly, until Brahk made a loop with the thumb and forefinger on his left hand and inserted the index of his right into the resultant hole. He made squeaking and moaning noises as the speed of his finger fornication increased. Sir Humperdinck's face turned to crimson, and he looked to his feet, his large boots moving side to side and kicking a pebble in childish embarrassment. "Hee, hee," he laughed.

"Wait, are you a virgin?" Verreth asked. Sir Humperdinck's embarrassment turned to rage.

"Of course not. I have bedded many a fair maiden in my time."

"Brahk say you lying. Brahk think you never see naked girl ever."

"I did too, once," the knight sputtered. "I once saw a maiden, bathing in a lake, clad only in shimmering samite."

"That's not naked," Verreth said.

"Well, she took it off." Sir Humperdinck countered. "As she was dipping into the water."

"So never saw naked then?" Brahk asked.

"No, technically not, but …"

"Ha, ha, no technically. You a virgin."

Sir Humperdinck's face flushed more, and he gripped the hilt of his sword in a tight grip.

"Enough, you idiots!" Serraia barked in a loud voice. "Help me bury him."

The three men, properly chastised, nodded and then looked down finding their feet to be very fascinating. Serraia stared at them for several long seconds, her jaw twitching in rage, daring each one to speak.

"Uh, Serraia," Brahk said, raising a hand like a child in a school room. Her eyes snapped to him and saw he was pointing down. She spun to see Gerryt's body was dissolving into a viscous soup, which then leched directly into the stone of the cavern floor.

A sound of despair came from her and she brought a hand to her mouth. Around them the bodies of the wyrmynn also turned to pools of steaming, bubbling goo. The organic slurry seeped into the floor. Not long after, the weapons and armor scattered across the floor disintegrated to dust.

"Fell sorcery indeed," Sir Humperdinck asked, covering his nose with the edge of his cloak to block the acidic smell of melting flesh. He looked to the others. "We must cleanse this place."

The others nodded with a renewed sense of purpose. A few minutes later they marched through the wyrmynn camp, ignoring the women and children in their pens, and descended to the next level.

As they stepped into a new chamber, they saw another dread knight turn and flee.

Back in the throne room, Simon cringed as he watched the Barrow feed. "That never stops being gross."

Is it any different from how you fed when you were alive?

the Barrow asked.

"Yes, yes, it is. I never dissolved my food and slurped it through a straw."

What is a straw?

"You know, I'm not quite sure. Not important though. Those assholes are on their way."

The remaining dread knight is leading them to the black ooze. Perhaps we will get lucky.

"Maybe," Simon said.

You do realize that you are speaking aloud again?

"Yeah, so?"

You know it is unnecessary.

"Yes, I know," Simon said, his voice sounding every bit like the petulant teenager he was. "But, this voice is growing on me."

If you say so, the Barrow said in a tone laced with sarcasm.

"You could stop being such a jerk."

You are right. I apologize.

"Um, good." Simon felt uncomfortable and spoke again. "How're your power levels looking?"

In response, the Barrow opened a status window in Simon's vision.

The Barrow.

Host: Simon.
Current Tier: 1
True Tier: 8
Health: 8,567/86,890.
Status: Starving.

Race: Sentient Dungeon

The Barrow is one of the most ancient sentient dungeons on all Korynn, but years of neglect have left it starving. Now that it has bound itself to a host it is capable of consuming energy and experiences.

Current Level Essence Points: 687.

"Not too shabby guy. We'll get you back up to Tier 2 in no time."

Assuming the Knight of the Blazing Fist does not kill you and force me to go dormant before that occurs.

"Yeah, how do we stop that from happening?"

We could hope for the best.

The best turned out to be not so great. The black ooze dissolved both the dread knight decoy and the half-orc, but it fled when the knight sent flashes of empyrean light blazing through the chamber. The rest of the adventurers pressed on as the Barrow absorbed the two corpses.

"Was it just me or did the black ooze kinda look like a dude?" Simon asked.

Indeed, it is a curious form for the creature to take.

"It kinda looked familiar too, but I can't quite place it."

That is a mystery for another time.

"Right. At least Spinny turned them away from the dark dryad's grove."

I'm not sure that was the best strategy.

"Saving her life wasn't the best strategy?"

No. She could have killed a few more of them. And if she fell, she would have provided a filling meal. Either way, we are weaker for protecting her. But you want a date.

"You are one cold bastard."

I am as my nature defines me, as are you, as is this Knight of the Blazing fist. I fear your sentimentality may doom us both.

In a typical teenage fashion, Simon refused to admit the Barrow was right, and he was wrong. "Well, no point in crying over spilled milk. What do we do now?"

The only thing we can do. Generate as many dread knights as possible and hope.

"No," Simon said. "There is one more thing we can do. I'll need a bit of that power of yours."

8

Sir Humperdinck led them through the final hallway and into the Barrow King's throne room. The undead sorcerer sat on his throne, black spectral smoke robes flowed around him and he clutched a gnarled staff of blackened wood. An unnerving chill flowed in waves through the room, biting into Verreth's bones.

Arrayed in front of the lich were more than a dozen dread knights. These were better armed and armored, and fuller in the muscle department than the ones they'd dispatched earlier.

"I do not like this," Serraia said.

"Fear not fair maiden, for I am Sir Herman Heinrich Humperdinck and I was born for this moment. I hold my sword up high, bathed in the glory and light of the empyrean realm. I will lay these abominations low and I..."

"Jeez dude, are you done yet?" the Barrow King asked.

Sir Humperdinck stopped and looked in shock and bewilderment at the undead monstrosity who'd just interrupted him. "How... how dare you?"

"Yeah, yeah, I dare. You're boring. Shut up."

Verreth looked sideways at Serraia and whispered. "He sounds like a kid?"

The Barrow King's eyes snapped to Verreth, and all the arrogance and confidence leached from him like blood from a critical wound.

"Um, no I am not a kid. I am the Barrow King, and I'm many, many thousands of years old. And powerful. You don't know how powerful."

"Okay," Verreth said, leaning back on one foot, prepping to run if the need arose.

"I care not how much power you have, for I, Sir Herman ..."

"Harry Humperjohnson, yeah, yeah I know, I heard you the first time," The Barrow King said, once again interrupting the knight.

"Well... I never. It is Heinrich Humperdinck not ... I won't even repeat what you said." The knight sputtered and wheezed as he tried to regain his composure.

Verreth grew suspicious. Something was off with this whole situation. What he didn't know was whether that 'off' worked to his benefit, or if it meant his doom was upon him. He needed more information.

"If I may, your liege?" Verreth asked, earning an angry glare from Sir Humperdinck for daring to address the Barrow King. "I believe we can come to a beneficial arrangement."

The Barrow King turned its silvery eyed gaze upon him. "Yeah? Whatcha thinkin'?"

"Well, as you may suspect, my lovely companion and I do not see eye to eye with all of our stalwart companion's ... philosophies."

"What?" Sir Humperdinck blurted in shock, eyes glaring at Verreth. "He is a lord of undeath, a foul defiler of life and ... and ... he speaks in a mocking tone."

"Yeah, I don't care about any of that," Verreth said. "I just want to live."

"You cannot be serious," Serraia said, eyes tinged with red. "He killed Gerryt."

"I did not. That was the wyrmynn," The Barrow King protested, leaning forward, hand clutching his staff. "Though we did feed on his corpse, so I get why you're mad." The Barrow King eased back onto his throne and made a sound like a man struggling to suck a piece of mutton from between his teeth. "Sorry, I'm still getting used to these new teeth." He sucked for a few more seconds. "Almost got it." The slurping grew to a disgusting intensity.

"We are wasting time," Sir Humperdinck roared and raised his sword. "I call on the Devas of Light and the Lords of Life to grant me the power to burn this dread revenant of death."

Golden light flared from every pore of Sir Humperdinck's body. Verreth watched as it flowed over the closest dread knight charring its skin. The other dread knights leapt into battle even though each moment of exposure to the knight's holy light burned away more of their artificial life.

The Barrow King raised his staff and smacked it hard on the dais in front of his throne. A shimmering shield expanded in front of the revenant glistening like an oil-covered puddle. The empyrean energy impacted the shield with the force of a stormfront against a rocky shore, but the shield held.

The dread knights were not so lucky. The holy energy rolled over and through them. Then the light flashed out, leaving multicolored spots lingering in everyone who had eyes.

Verreth blinked away the spots just in time to see the dread knights collapse in heaps of ash.

"Well that sucked," The Barrow King said, a twinge of fear pushing through the pubescent squeak in his voice. "You couldn't have waited a few more seconds to do that?"

"Why would I deign to grant you even a second more of this unnatural existence?" Sir Humperdinck asked.

"Because then my reinforcements could have arrived."

Sir Humperdinck had no time to wonder what the Barrow King was talking about before a wave of high-pitched keening erupted into the room in the form of dozens of tiny, mushroom-headed men. Several of the fungoid creatures rammed their toadstool caps into the back of Sir Humperdinck's legs, knocking him to the ground.

A dozen more of the creatures swarmed the downed knight, bursts of spores exploding from mouthlike orifices straight into his face. The knight howled in pain and confusion, struggling to regain his feet. He swung his massive sword back and forth, cleaving through the spongy bodies of the mushroom men with ease.

Verreth grabbed Serraia's arm as he backed away from the expanding cloud of spores but could not pull her free before the spores enveloped her head. She hacked and coughed and then screamed.

Verreth released his grip on her and fell backward, scrabbling on all fours to the back wall where he hid behind a column. He watched as Serraia's tanned skin became a splotchy melange of gray-green spots. She went silent and fell onto her face.

Another roar of pain and anger drew Verreth's gaze back to Sir Humperdinck. He rose to one knee, swung his sword wide, ending the life of three more mushroom men, then stood and swung again. The surviving fungoid creatures backed away, possessing enough self-awareness to preserve their lives.

Sir Humperdinck held his free hand up and made a fist. A corona of green fire flowed around his fist, up his arm and surrounded his entire body. Then the green flames thrummed off of the knight's body in waves. A high-pitched keening rose from the fungoid men as the green fire rolled over them and they started burning, bringing the pleasant smell of roasted mushrooms to Verreth's nose. The waves of green fire did not penetrate the Barrow King's shield, but it flickered and then failed as the wave of green fire dissipated.

Sir Humperdinck knelt, placed his sword point down and spoke.

"A Knight of the Blazing Fist is the light in the darkness, a shield for the living and the bane of the undead. Your foul existence is at an end. I will cleave thy skull in twain. I will sunder your connection to this realm and cast your tortured soul to the abyss. While I have breath left in my lungs and while my beating heart pumps lifeblood through me, I shall let no undead live. This I vow."

Sir Humperdinck stood, surrounded by holy fire and filled with radiant light. He strode with purpose towards the undead lord.

"I just have one thing I'd like to ask," the Barrow King said, the pitch of his voice rising.

"I will hear none of your foul incantations, lich," Sir Humperdinck said and swung his sword in a mighty arc. The Barrow King ducked, and the sword missed by mere inches, taking a chunk of bone out of his throne.

"No, no incantations, just a question, one of theology."

"I have no interest in what you have to say. The knight swung again, and this time the strike caused the lich to fall onto its backside.

"I was wondering if that vow you made is binding?"

"Of course, it is. I am a knight, and I live and die by my honor." He swung again, the sword slicing through one of the

204

Barrow King's arms. The Barrow King screamed as the limb fell away, dissolving into ectoplasmic goo before it hit the ground.

"I only ask, cuz I noticed that you're not breathing."

Oh crap, Verreth thought, a deep unease growing in his stomach.

"What?" Sir Humperdinck blurted, causing his swing to miss its mark.

"You're not breathing," the Barrow King said. "And your heart isn't beating. You realize you are undead ... right?"

Sir Humperdinck stopped his next attack, letting his sword clang to the ground. His eyes widened and his mouth hung open. "What?" he said rather stupidly. His mouth may not have known the truth, but his eyes did and his fingers went limp and his sword clattered to the ground. He fell to his knees and beseeching eyes looked up, locking onto the silver glows inside the Barrow King's skull.

"Yeah, sorry dude. I thought you knew," the Barrow King said.

"I'm dead."

"Undead, hence why you can still walk around and threaten and such."

"I am the evil I despise."

"Come on guy. It's not that bad, really. Beats the alternative, right?"

Sir Humperdinck wept, his shoulders pumping up and down as ragged sobs flowed through him. After a moment he calmed, grabbed his sword and stood. The Barrow King backed away, but Sir Humperdinck did not attack. Instead, he looked at the lich with eyes that begged forgiveness. After a moment he looked away.

"I cannot live as one of the accursed undead," the knight said in a low voice, and then swung his sword at his own neck. The blade bounced off his shoulder, deflected by the pauldrons of his armor. He tried again, and again, with no further success. Chopping off one's own head was apparently harder than it looked. After a few more tries, Sir Humperdinck fell to his knees and wept.

The Barrow King knelt by the knight's side. After a moment he placed a spectral hand on the dead knight's shoulder. "If you need someone to talk to, I'm a good listener."

"I just want to die."

"Yeah, saw that. Kinda hard to do it that way though."

Sir Humperdinck looked up at the Barrow King. "Will you help me?"

"Uh … you sure you don't wanna hang around? We could be pals."

"I just want to die."

"Suit yourself then."

Verreth watched as the Barrow King stood, picked up Sir Humperdinck's sword and gave it a few practice swings. The revenant nodded in appreciation as Sir Humperdinck knelt, grabbing the sides of the throne and exposing his neck.

"I hope you find what you're looking for," the Barrow King said in an unexpectedly kind voice and brought the sword down in one quick, terrible blow.

Sir Humperdinck's head plopped onto the seat of the throne and his body slumped to the floor. The tin amulet slipped from the neck stump and clattered to the floor. The Barrow King bent down and picked it up. Then it began to glow.

"Woah, what the…?" the Barrow King shouted, dropping the amulet.

The amulet bounced and hummed and spun. It gyrated faster and faster and then imploded into a singularity. The singularity pulsed and frothed and then suddenly a corpulent man, naked as the day he was born, popped into existence.

"Ahhh," the Barrow King said in a tone most unbecoming of a lord of the undead and watched as the man moaned, vomited and then collapsed onto his face. The singularity stopped spinning, expanded back into the amulet and thunked off the newcomer's head and clattered to a stop a few inches from the Barrow King's foot.

"Who the hell is this guy?" the Barrow King blurted.

Verreth didn't know what was going on with the Barrow King. He was nothing like the ancient tales suggested, even accounting for the exaggeration and liberal treatment of facts those tales often fell victim to. It was time to gamble with the prize being his life.

"It was a curse," Verreth said.

"Oh, shit, I forgot you were there," the Barrow King said jumping. He stared right at Verreth and despite the creature's juvenile nature, Verreth felt his blood chill. "You know who this dude is?"

"I do. His name is Bahldreck, he's the least favorite son of a minor local noble family, and he unwittingly carried the burden of that family's curse."

"Tell me about this curse."

"His family was once very powerful, but they reneged on a promise to help the Knights of the Blazing Fist, leading to all but one member of the order being killed right here in the Barrow. The lone survivor used powerful magic to bind the soul of one of their greatest warriors to the amulet." Verreth pointed at the amulet.

The Barrow King stopped, gingerly picking it up. "Did Bahldreck deserve the burden?"

"No, by all accounts he was a good guy."

"Yet you still used him?"

"I did," Verreth said. "I never said I was a good guy."

Bahldreck moaned and opened and closed his mouth like a suffocating fish.

"Is he gonna be okay?" the Barrow King asked.

"Do you care?" Verreth asked.

"I don't like bullies," the Barrow King said, looking down upon Bahldreck.

A shock moved through Verreth's body as a realization hit him. "Someone did this to you," he said, and it wasn't a question.

The Barrow King looked up, eyes drilling into Verreth's soul. This wasn't hyperbole. He felt his soul being analyzed, parsed and cataloged. Verreth had never been so afraid in his life.

"You have one chance to walk out of here with your life," the Barrow King said in a voice that was much surer than it had been.

Verreth froze. "I'm listening."

"Maybe you've figured it out already, but I'm kinda new here. I took over from the last asshole and I'm looking to do things differently from the way he did them. I'm a people person."

"You mean you eat people," Verreth said, hoping he hadn't overplayed his hand.

"That's not technically correct. The Barrow doesn't eat people, it dissolves those who die in its environs and absorbs their energy and experiences. But I can see how that bit of minutia wouldn't make much of a difference to you."

"It makes me feel better, oddly."

"Good, that means we might be able to work together."

"What do you have in mind?" Verreth asked, a whiff of hope pushing through his feelings of dread.

"I'm looking to expand. But, I have a marketing problem, being a murderous dungeon who consumes people and all."

"And you want me to what, convince people to come here?"

"The right kind of people."

"And what kind of people is that?"

"The strong kind. Like you. You came here. You must have had a reason?"

Verreth nodded. "Treasure."

"I suspected as much. I can provide people with a chance to achieve their dreams of wealth and power, but I want you to vet them?"

"Vet them?" Verreth asked.

"I will not continue the tradition of the powerful preying on the weak. I will not allow lords and slavers to send people in here against their will so they may reap the benefits of their slaughter. Any man or woman, or shambling bit of fungus may enter the Barrow of their own accord. Some will get their treasure, others will die and feed us, but it will be fair."

Verreth buried his surprise, sensing an opportunity, not only to extend his lifespan but to increase the size of his coin purse. "You want me to be your gatekeeper?"

"I was thinking the Grand Poobah of Awesome, but your title sounds more official."

"What's in it for me?" Verreth asked

"Apart from your life?" The Barrow King stared at him until Verreth nodded. "You get to tax those you bring to the Barrow at a rate of 10% of all the swag they take, with the caveat that any weapons, armor or other items that specialize in killing, protecting people from or even mildly inconveniencing the undead are mine. What do you say?"

Verreth's heart thudded in his chest. In all his years of hustling, cheating, and scheming, he'd never imagined a moment like this one. He looked up at the Barrow King. "Make it 15% and we have a deal."

The Barrow King stared for several long heartbeats, and Verreth feared he had overplayed his hand when the Barrow King extended a spectral hand that turned to bone. "Done."

Verreth hesitated for the merest of moments before he reached forward and took the hand. A chill pushed into his bones. *I'm going to live,* he thought and realized that until that moment he truly believed he would die. He looked up at the undead horror and smiled.

"The name's Verreth."

"Good to meet ya man, I'm Simon."

THE END